G. Albert Aurier

ELSEWHERE

AND OTHER STORIES

Translated and with an Introduction by

Brian Stableford

CONTENTS

INTRODUCTION

GABRIEL-ALBERT AURIER (1865-1892), who usually employed the signature G.-Albert Aurier but occasionally signed himself Georges-Albert Aurier, was an ardent and very active member of the Symbolist Movement during the years immediately prior to his premature death from typhus. He is primarily remembered nowadays as an art critic, especially as a vociferous early advocate of the work of Vincent van Gogh and Paul Gauguin.

Aurier was a contributor to *Le Décadent* before launching his own periodical, *Le Moderniste illustré* in 1889. He published a small collection of poetry, *L'Oeuvre maudit*, in 1889, and a novel, *Vieux*, in 1891, before his career was cut tragically short. He assisted in the founding of the *Mercure de France*, where his most famous essays on painters appeared, and the press associated with that periodical published a collection of *Oeuvres posthumes* in 1893. That volume included numerous works derived from manuscripts that he had not had the opportunity to place with publishers while he was alive, most notably the "novel"—perhaps more accurately describable as a novella—"Ailleurs" (here translated as "Elsewhere"), his masterpiece, completed shortly before his death and accidentally anticipatory of it.

All but one of the stories contained in the present collection were included in *Oeuvres posthumes*, although one of them, "L'Amante" (tr. as "The Lover") had been published previously in the second issue of *Le Moderniste illustré*, 4 mai 1889. The other story included herein, "Festin de Balthazar" (tr. as "Belshazzar's Feast") had appeared in the first issue of that periodical, dated 27 avril 1889—the first issue—under the heading *Fantaisie*. Two of the prose poems were untitled in *Oeuvres posthumes* because the manuscripts from which they were taken had no titles, but I have taken the liberty of attaching the titles "The Blue Woman" and "Pride" to them.

The title that Aurier chose for his periodical was by no means the first attempt to define "modernism" in art, and the word has accumulated so many retrospective meanings and applications since that it has become very slippery indeed, but by almost any definition, "Ailleurs" is an important work of modernist prose fiction, determinedly original in its narrative method, casually self-referential while deliberately avoiding explanation of the peculiar symbolism of its violent climax. In its declared intention to present an autobiography that dismisses real events as irrelevant in order to focus on the imaginary, and in its caustic admixture of the earnest and the satirical in its defiant championship of the poetic in opposition to the assaults of positivistic science, it is a significant precursor of surrealism. Although it has affinities, unsurprisingly, with other near-contemporary radical Symbolist texts, notably Adolphe Retté's *Thulé des brumes* (1891; tr. as *Misty Thule*) and the works of Charles Morice, Jules Laforgue and Alfred Jarry, "Ailleurs" is very much one of a kind, and has lost none of its trenchancy with the passage of time.

The shorter works appended to the novella in the present volume are best regarded as experimental endeavors testing out new directions in Symbolist short fiction. "Aveline" is an ironic response to Catulle Mendès paradisal fantasies, which had begun to appear in newspapers in the mid-1890s before being juxtaposed in his collections with slyly risqué vignettes of contemporary Parisian life, of a kind that Aurier similarly attempts to outdo in "L'Aieule" (tr. as "The Ancestress") and "Festin de Balthazar." The brutal economy of his satire is well illustrated in "Plutus" and the idiosyncratic ambiguity of his symbolism in "The Blue Woman," although both traits show up in more elaborately stylish fashion in his flamboyant poetry. As to how he might have been able to build on those foundation stones we can only speculate, but there is more than enough originality and pugnacious opposition to convention even in his finger-exercises to license regret for the fact that he did not live to do more, and "Ailleurs" offers abundant proof of the loss that the Symbolist Movement suffered when he died.

The translations of the first six items in the collection were made from the copy of *Oeuvres posthumes* reproduced in the Bibliothèque Nationale's *gallica* website. The translations of the remaining two stories were made from copies of *Le Moderniste illustré* reproduced on *gallica*.

—Brian Stableford

ELSEWHERE

AND OTHER STORIES

ELSEWHERE

*T*HIS *is the story of Hans.*

You have doubtless never heard of him, for he spent the entirety of his short life far away from Paris, far away from France, on the Moon, where he was also born.

When he died on 16 February 1890 he left me in his handwritten will the manuscript of this strange work, and the responsibility of having it published.

I have limited myself to translating it as faithfully as possible from Selenian into French. If I have not clarified with commentaries the evident obscurity of this singular book, that is because, I must confess, I scarcely understood certain passages of it myself, and the general idea of the work still escapes me completely. I have preferred to rely upon the intelligence of the reader, who, more sagacious than me, I am sure, will easily clarify the matters that embarrass me.

The Translator.

I believe that my name is Hans.

I have conceived the project of writing a novel, which will be my story.

Do not be astonished if this novel does not resemble others. I live in a land where that genre of literature is unknown. I only know of its existence by virtue of the testimony of a few travelers, who have furnished me with details on that subject, by which I am greatly astonished.

The subject of my novel will be what certain novelists known as realists attempt to produce, I am told: a slice of life, a slice of my life.

Yes, I will write the story of some of the years that I have lived. How? I don't know, and what does it matter?

During those years, what happened to me? Nothing. Besides which, I am convinced that nothing has ever happened to anyone. Never. Never . . .

For, quite frankly, one cannot consider as adventures the fact of being variously tossed about by the viscous and poisonous liquid of life in which we float.

If, however, you adhere to that conventional fashion of speaking, I could say that banal things have happened to me, as they do to everyone, the memory of which I have lost . . .

"What a singular hero of a novel you make!" you might say to me.

Alas, I only recall the dreams that I have dreamed.

But dreams do not come alone. They are always determined by those accidents of life that you are reproaching me for having forgotten, and they are determined logically.

If, therefore, I write the story of my dreams for you, you will be able without difficulty, I imagine—since it is the only thing that interests you—to reconstruct the banal story of my real life. I will not lie to you, for, I swear to you, I have forgotten it . . . forgotten . . . forgotten . . .

Doubtless, this fashion of writing a novel, this fashion of writing one's life by only recounting the unreal, the ideal reflexity, is strange and far from the fashion of certain accredited novelists who, I am assured, content themselves with recounting the material existences of their personages, to the extent of informing you of the menu of their meals and the nature of their evacuations. Nevertheless, perhaps . . .

And then, doubtless, as is affirmed, I am strange, and dissimilar to other people.

But then, might it not be true that that very dissimilarity might interest someone?

Personally, I am glad to be able to believe that I am dissimilar to others, in order to be able to hope to interest myself.

I do not recall where and when I was born. I only recall that, out there, in that old little village where I grew up, and of which I no longer know the name, in the utmost depths of a great mysterious cathedral, whose ogives seemed to be doors open to paradise, as many sparkling and celestial sumptuoussnesses of stained glass, in its utmost depths, in the little chapel of the month of Mary, on a beautiful silver altar florid with white bouquets, among the candles at the ex-votos, there was a beautiful, miraculous Madonna.

She was clad in heavy brocade fabrics, like a Byzantine Empress, covered in precious stones. Golden stars constellated her azure robe. A luminous nimbus aureoled her divine head. She was holding between her fingers the stem of a blooming lily. Her face was milder and prettier, certainly, than one can say. Benevolent smiles, like tireless birds, fluttered in the melancholy sky of her gaze.

She—I remember it clearly—was my first lover. Oh, I was a child then, very young, and every evening, in the great mysterious cathedral, I knelt down piously at her feet and recited madrigals, encouraged by the immutable indulgent smile and her gaze: chaste and mystical madrigals, as humble and as soft as prayers.

I only implored her for the grace of being able to contemplate her for longer, the grace of seeing my ineffable amour welcomed by a smile, and I was happy, very happy, happier than one can say, for I always found in the immutable indulgent smile of her beautiful eyes the mute acquiescence to my timid prayers.

Alas, how all that felicity crumbled! Why did I not remain a child, a happy little child satisfied with his adoration and the mystical smiles of the Good Lady?

An evening came—a sacrilegious evening, after which I wept, after which my teeth ground in an insatiable desire—an unforeseen evening of dementia, in which my young fingers wanted to touch the beautiful azure robe constellated with golden stars.

Oh, since that sacrilegious evening, how many tears I have shed, how much bitter disgust I have swallowed, without extinguishing the ardent thirst of my filthy desires! And henceforth, no doubt, I shall weep more, I shall bewail forever the crime of having stolen the garter of the Madonna in a moment of unforeseen dementia.

❋

After the fatal evening when I stole the Madonna's garter, I ran through the city, I ran like a famished dog.

The memory of my sacrilege pursued me. The clear vision of the impious act always loomed up before me. I saw once again my hands, trembling with fever, reaching out toward the azure robe constellated with gold, clenching hesitantly, recoiling, then returning, then madly lifting the brocade fabrics, lifting those heavy and stiff blue skirts, and, with a demented gesture, unfastening the blue satin garter . . .

And the heavy and stiff blessed skirts fell back . . .

Too late, alas! Had I not had time to perceive, with a frisson of my entire being, in the shadow, above the stocking of woven gold and silver, a scintillation of pink marble that was flesh?

Oh, since that fatal evening, how I have run around the city, how I have run, a poor dog hungry for that glimpsed flesh.

It was always at night, almost always on nights of squalls and rain. They were prowling the boulevards in the black mud, their eyes begging, their gestures imploring, their necks suppliant, the miserable bitches with the bodies of women. They tucked up their skirts all the way to the thighs, and the mud speckled their white stockings with black . . .

Or, at other times, it was under ceilings with garish gildings, in places of dolorous joy, under the streaming of bright lights. They strove to smile without cracking the plaster with which their sepulchral faces were blanched, to fluff up their furbelows, hypocritical tabernacles hiding from the eyes the putrescence of their bodies . . .

And all of them made no protest, any more than the Madonna had, when my famished hands and my famished eyes violated the mystery of their robes, and they all smiled indifferently when my voracious teeth of a young dog went for the spoils of their flesh.

Did they really not know that I was partaking of that repulsive feast, in which they had served up, in vulgar or precious dishes, the meat of their own bodies, with my jaws bitter and my belly unsated, weeping with rage and disgust and, alas, even more with desire and hunger?

Was it true then, that it was necessary not to know? That the man who had known love could no longer love? That he could never savor again the ineffable felicity in the smiling eyes of the Madonna, the man who has touched her brocade skirts with his finger?

Then why had God given us fingers, and why had he given her, the eternal Madonna, sparkling flesh like pink marble, and why had he put in our hearts, the enemy of the love that purifies, the love that soils, the love that dirties, that shameful desire for kisses that it is necessary to wash off as soon as one has received them?

Oh, I understand the Biblical fable now: ignorance is the luminous paradise of joy, and knowledge is the baleful night of dolor and anguish, but the eternal serpent is always coiled in the branches of the mystical orange tree and, an eternal victorious tempter, always drags humankind far from the luminous paradise of joy, into the baleful night of dolor and anguish.

And I too, like Eve, groan for having learned, I groan for having listened to the serpent speak, and I search in vain in the night for the soft, good, blue stars that were the smiling eyes of the Madonna.

Oh, is there no redemption for that inevitable sin? Could I not, by bathing myself in some fabulous Lethe, forget, forget everything, return to my primal candor, to the joys of my puerile ignorance?

※

"Poor child! Don't despair. A redemption exists."

"Where can I find it?"

"In yourself."

"I haven't found anything in myself but despair and disgust."

"No! Descend into your soul. Your soul, child, is a garden as florid as Eden, where the Lethe flows that you implored. An eternally blue sky is mirrored there in eternally blue lakes. There are pink mountains, grasslands, moss, marvelous flowers and laburnum woods. Descend into your soul, child, and walk in that chosen land, at the hazard of your whim, in search of happiness. It is there alone that you will find it! If you try to emerge from yourself, you will only encounter disappointment, bitterness and disgust."

"Master, will I rediscover in the beautiful landscapes of my soul the Madonna whose smiling gaze alone can save me from despair?"

"Child, march through life with eyes closed and take by the hand the first woman who bumps into you. Take her by the hand and invite her to descend into the beautiful landscapes that I have revealed to you. What does it matter that she might have the rags of a beggar, an ugly face, gray hair or a vulgar mind? Bathe her in the enchanted lakes of your soul, and she will metamorphose in the radiant Madonna that you desire."

"Do I have such a power within me then without knowing it? Am I carrying an entire universe within my flesh?"

"A universe, child, greater and more beautiful than the universe! A universe of which you are the God!"

Oh, I can't do it, I can't! Will I ever be able to follow that advice to descend within myself, to live within myself, to close my eyes to the turpitudes that swarm around my flesh?

I have tried to march through life with my eyes closed, as the good mage told me. I have tried to take the hand of many women who bumped into me and invite them to descend into the florid gardens. But I have always opened my eyes too soon, and my heart has risen up in disgust.

Today, like yesterday, I was sad, but I am sad tonight with a materially dolorous sadness. The emptiness, the silence and the loneliness frighten me. Oh, how small and stupid the city is. The boulevards are already deserted, empty of the imbeciles and the vain figurants that encumbered them a few hours ago: empty, desolately empty; and the light of the moon falls onto things as sullen and dirty and as cold as winter rain, as melted snow. I've been wandering for eternities and I no longer know whether I can still speak. Perhaps I'm mute . . .

I have gone into night cafés . . . they're noisy and luminous, but I can see that they're only putting on a semblance of not sleeping. There are Edison lamps that play with the false gold of cardboard moldings, and jets of water that piss among zinc rushes in basins of fake porphyry, and an infinity of people who talk Wallachian while eating sauerkraut and crayfish.

And yet, it's better than the frightfully mute night of a bedroom.

But why stay in this city of mud and disgust? I've departed for distant regions, hoping to find peace and calm in the azure and verdure. I went to the château of the engineer Bildebières, counting on finding self-satisfaction there, and everything that characterizes that savant friend.

"Oh, how good it is of you to have come!" cried the engineer Bildebières, as soon as I leapt out of the tilbury.

"Oh what a pleasant surprise," said Madame Bilde-bières, simpering at me.

And men in flannel jackets and women in bright dresses saluted me ceremoniously with their panama hats and multicolored umbrellas.

I wanted to weep.

It was in the lush countryside, in the park with the old sullen beeches and pale plane trees; they went forth, all of them, conversing idly under bright umbrellas or panama hats, their strolls circling in the immutable cage of the park with the old sullen beeches and the pale plane trees. They wandered, sowing futile words and laughter. The men, under the panamas, drooled words of practical agriculture, and the women, under the bright umbrellas, jabbered phrases about questions of clothes or trousseaus, or sniggered at gossip reported from the nearby little town. Every morning, every morning, and until evening, in the park with the sullen old beeches and the pale plane trees, they go forth like that, all of them, talking like that and laughing like that, under the bright umbrellas or the panamas.

And as that bleak parade was repeated for numerous days, and I couldn't muster any enthusiasm for their vain chirping, and as I maintained the grim silence of a rock in their midst, it happened that the visual senses were exaggerated within me, and I ended up seeing distinctly the inside of the heads of those men and women who were wandering in the park of old sullen beeches and pale plane trees. I saw the interior of their heads distinctly. There was—yes, I remember—a little ball of gray broth surrounded by a thick bony carapace. And at each word they proffered, the bony carapace was augmented and the ball of gray broth diminished proportionately. I saw that distinctly. The ball of gray broth diminished, diminished, diminished. Some of them already had nothing in the center of the head but an immensely hard and dense bony ball, like a billiard ball. And that was in the park with the old sullen beeches and the pale plane trees; it was sad enough to make one weep.

It was necessary to come back, having not been able to talk either with the azure or the verdure; it was necessary to come back to the city and resume dragging one's feet and one's thoughts through the immutable mud, and recommencing the lamentable métier of a stray dog.

Did I not attempt in those days to utilize the hours in tasks? Did I not attempt to interest myself in gestures of my hands, and efforts of my intelligence? Did I not try to polish a cane, solve a problem in mechanics, decipher the rebus in an illustrated paper, or write a poem?

What was the point? My arms fell back, inert, and my thoughts melted into a dolorous fog, and for the first time, I understood the pointlessness of living, the imbecility of living, and perhaps I leaned over the parapet of the river, gazing at the black water flowing with the lugubrious and silent splashing made of the sobs of all the dolorous people who seek peace there? Perhaps I leaned over desirously . . . ?

But was I not afraid of that unknown? Was it not fear that suggested that I attempt a new experiment, to march again into the night in search of the creature who would descend into the beautiful gardens of which the mage spoke, and who would become the Madonna of my time of ignorance, and whose lips would pour me the forgotten happiness?

Oh, now, miserable coward, now I am far from the black river whose whispers called to me, and I am running around the city in fête and fleeing the dark streets for luminous elsewheres. And I have fallen down, exhausted and discouraged . . .

And there is, again, as always, under that banal heraldic ceiling and amid the sadism without distinction of that unclerical stained glass, the same prideful noise of the crowd, the same inane splashing of the ocean—an ocean in which the waves are grotesquely anthropomorphic . . . my sick uncle's sea-baths! Something, in truth, like a psychological Trouville.

Mounted in old sculpted oak, the faded verdure, the drunken dwarfs and the heavy hop-fueled gaiety of the worn Flanders tapestries display the entire scale of their calm faded tints on the walls in the sharp diamond radiance of an Edison lamp, a cold and brutal star. That dissonance enchants me. It enchants me as much as, in all that Gothic furniture, the little chocolate bombs and the disquieting jet-cylinders that ornament the host of occiputs, as many cigarettes fuming between the excessively scarlet lips of the women, out there, as sumptuous and plastered as façades . . .

Why should I be embarrassed and not repeat that . . . my soul has colic. Such confessions imply ridicule and mockery, I know. In what way, however, are those simple words more grotesque than the sublimities of Aeschylus?

"You'll bring me what I need to write, won't you . . . ?"

To write? What's the point? What's the point, in sum? Are the anthropomorphic waves not unfurling over the epidermis of my soul? I'm in the bath. Why, then, would I write? And for whom? To whom? How do I know? But it's necessary! Certainly, it's necessary. Oh, the eternal priapism of the writing desk! Look at them, lounging in the peace of long swallowings. Doubtless, by virtue of a slow endomosis, their liquid brains are trickling away, gradually, with the beer they've drunk. They're trickling into their bellies, their liquid brains, all the way to the urinals . . .

Personally, now, I feel as if myriads of the torturous feet of flies are tickling my quivering and capillary nerves, and my marrows, and my fibers, and all the cells of my brain—especially those of the circumvolutions near the fissure of Rolando,[1] where, as everyone knows, Hetzig[2] has localized the psycho-motor centers. Oh, that martyrdom! And them, drinking and digesting . . . I can hear their stomachs functioning quite clearly . . . but it seems to me that, from one minute to the next, their skulls are diminishing, diminishing, diminishing . . .

Why, then, am I convinced that the mathematical resultant of all these infimal vibrations that the above-mentioned feet of the flies are imprinting on my nervous system constitutes a very curious, and even grandiose, physical phenomenon, like, for instance, a cyclone or an aurora borealis? Why, also, do I esteem that all these people who surround me ought to be admiring this spectacle, assuredly very banal, open-mouthed, with the satisfaction of English tourists who have seen a fine cataclysm . . . ?

---

1 The fissure of Ronaldo, once so-called after the neurophysiologist Luigi Ronaldo (1773-1831) is nowadays known as the central sulcus; it separates the parietal lobe of the brain from the frontal lobe, where the primary motor cortex is located.

2 The mistaken reference is to Éduard Hitzig (1838-1907), who made the cited attribution in collaboration with Gustav Frisch (1837-1927).

But now they're all laughing, and their laughter makes me indignant and desolates me, like a blasphemy, or rather, an insolent imbecility!

Certainly, all that is far from being obvious . . .

In any case, the mysterious endomosis is accomplishing its work. As I had already observed in the country in the guests of the engineer Bildebières, from one minute to the next, the skulls are diminishing, diminishing, diminishing . . .

Hold on! That Monsieur over there already has no head . . . no, no more head at all . . .

Oh, how they're bruising my soul, all these ambient etroides,[1] who don't appear to feel and who, in fact, don't feel the monstrous torture of the flies' feet. My entire body is vibrating dolorously, as if vibrating under the bow of a hyperesthetic double-bass . . .

Over there, in a corner, I glimpse three young boys, virginal and too pink, smiling and pulling faces. They are adroitly heightened with pastel, and their lips with water-color. Their fingernails are polished like those of abbés, and their phalanges sport proud circlets of gold. Their jackets, congruously shortened, uncover voluptuous, almost Hottentot callipygias.

But now I think about it, perhaps those three young boys have infamous mores . . .

At any rate, this imbecile crowd, this crowd of stupid individuals folded over their bellies, is beginning to give me nausea and, so to speak, sea-sickness.

---

1 This non-existent word does occur in a few nineteenth-century French texts, by virtue of the accidental running together of "et roides" [and stiff], and that is perhaps what the author intends to signify.

She, alone . . .

But then, why those smiles at the satisfied idiocy of her neighbor? Why the indulgence of her smiles to the indubitable goiter of her neighbor? Can she not see, then, the psychological goiter of her neighbor.

Oh, my God, after all, what logical induction is inciting me to conclude that her pale mauve eyes are anything but insensible opals, inapt to transmit sensations to her soul? Does she even have a soul? She prides herself on hair as blonde as hemp and slightly frizzy, doubtless by virtue of the artifice of curling-tongs That's all! Absolutely all . . . !

I can feel myself flowing, slowly into imbecility . . . the flies' feet are almost no longer making the double-bass of my body vibrate . . . *piano, piano, pianissimo*! Among the worn Flanders tapestries . . . oh, the little chocolate bombs . . . the endomosis . . . the callipygian voluptuousnesses . . . and Her! And her hair! And the rest . . . !

In sum, why all that? Let's reason . . . reason . . .

(A hole, a lacuna, a lethargy of consciousness. How long did it last?)

Now let's look. She's speaking. She has a long, quasi-aristocratic nose, and a wide, thin mouth, which is always laughing, as pale as a scar, in the middle of her paler face, her pseudo-Anglo-Saxon face, which doesn't know the solid joys of roast beef . . . and all that under her extraordinary yellow wig, fluffed up, as I've already said, by the dishonest artifices of curling-tongs.

Oh, the horrible clicking of dominoes . . . !

She isn't very young. No, undoubtedly, not very young! Unless she has no soul, which I don't know, nor even a God. Perhaps she has thirty-six juvenile autumns, or even forty, or perhaps a hundred, and more! But her skin is pale, and although somewhat dried out by the plaster, the bismuth, the magnesia and all the cosmetic gouache, without wrinkles visible to me, and her hair is blonde, as her soul must be, in the event, I repeat, that she has a soul, and I sense that if her little teeth weren't imperceptibly azured by the abuse of quicksilver, and if her pale mauve eyes, as cold and malicious as opals, weren't laughing with so much insistence, amid the dolorous and voluptuous hubbub of this stupid place, toward the monstrous goiter of her unqualifiable neighbor, perhaps one day she might be the Witch, the holy Witch, a thousand times blessed, whose divine philter . . .

"Messieurs, we're closing!"

About her, I dreamed about her, last night, all last night, her and her slightly long, quasi-aristocratic nose and the mysterious smile of her wide, thin mouth, palely pink, like a scar in the middle of a paler face, a pseudo-Anglo-Saxon face that doesn't know the solid joys of roast beef, and her extraordinary yellow wig, the color of honey, the color of hemp, fluffed up by the dishonest artifice of curling-tongs, and her teeth, imperceptible azured by the abuse of quicksilver, and her epidermis, slightly desiccated by plaster, bismuth, magnesia and all that cosmetic gouache, and most of all her eyes, her pale mauve eyes, as cold and malicious as opals and so discreet with regard to her soul.

I dreamed about her and, I don't know why, I called her Edwige, and for the first time in many years and many desires for women, I perceive that while desiring her violently, I didn't have, as is my constant habit, the dolorous desire for the disgusts of her flesh.

I considered her amorously, in my dream, almost as a sculptor considers, amorously, the repulsive lump of spoiled clay in which he reads, powerfully, the radiant poem of marble with which his soul is full.

Edwige, are you the one that I ought to take by the hand and lead, through the unexplored gardens, to the shore of the purificatory lakes?

The engineer Bildebières, returned from the country for a few days and, encountered at the corner of a boulevard, has taken me amicably by the arm and talked to me about the beauties of iron architecture and the imminent day when Notre-Dame, the Tour Saint-Jacques and the Pyramids of Egypt will be demolished, in order to be replaced by monuments a hundred times as high, of a less barbaric order, constructed entirely in metal, nickel-plated by means of a method of his own, permitting the avoidance of any oxidation.

"Oh, Monsieur Hans," he said to me, "nickel, nickel! What an admirable metal! You sometimes accuse engineers of neglecting the esthetic part of life, but on the contrary, we think about it! Think, then, about the dazzling effect that the gigantic monuments I'm talking about would have, nickel-plated from bottom to top, on a beautiful sunny day, clean, polished, glittering like gems. Imagine, then, what the aspect of future cities will be when everything, public monuments, private houses, the pavement of streets, are made of metal covered by a brilliant layer of nickel. Every morning, workers will furbish the façades, the roofs, the ground of the sidewalks and causeways; all that will shine, sparkle by day in the fires of the sun and by night in the glow of a thousand electric lamps.

"Nickel, Monsieur Hans, nickel, that metal so disdained that I know of considerable mines that are unexploited, will become, I tell you the basis of the ornamentation of future cities, and in truth, admit it, that will be cleaner and more beautiful than all your old sculpted stone and all your wretched painting . . . !"

Suddenly, I started. It was Her, Edwige.

"Even the tree trunks will be nickel-plated," the engineer added, semi-facetiously.

"What do you think of that woman going by?" I asked him.

"Pooh!" he said, "neither good nor bad. Ten years ago she might perhaps have been pretty. And then, you know, me, in the matter of women, I only like tall, very plump women. I want to have value for my money."

"She has strange eyes, simultaneously transparent and opaque, like opals, eyes as mysterious as gems, enigmatic eyes that mock with a smile anyone curious about her soul. Do you think she has a soul?"

"With you," the engineer replied, "there's never any means of talking seriously."

Under the tall trees, bored by always sheltering the same jets of water, the same geraniums, the same marble statues and the same children's nurses, in the great banal square, I have, after many hesitations, many vanquished timidities, succeeded in reaching the fugitive, the desired Edwige, and after many skirmishes, laughing at her little pretences of honesty, which want to appear frightened, I have seen her smile at me, and her hand, which I have taken, has not fled mine.

"I would love," I said to her, "I would love your name to be Edwige."

"Why?" she asked.

"Because that is what I baptized you on the night that I dreamed about you for the first time. There is a mysterious relationship between material forms and names, quasi-material forms of the same ideas, and a delicate soul can't abide seeing a term of that triple relationship broken. Delightful as the name might be that you have borne until now, that name, for me, is nasty and ugly if it isn't the name Edwige."

She looked at me with her strange mauve eyes, as mysterious as opals, without my being able to divine the thought that that enigmatic smile concealed; and she said:

"Well then, call me Edwige."

"If you wish, Edwige," I said to her another day, in that same banal square, "if you would like to allow yourself to be taken by the hand, and allow yourself to be guided by me, I would take you to marvelous elsewheres. Have you never dreamed of being suddenly transported far from your life, of no longer being, for a few moments, yourself?"

"Of course, but isn't it unrealizable?"

"No, but it's necessary to confide yourself to me; it's necessary for you to abandon yourself to me, without fear, without resistance, passively. I'll insufflate other souls, other lives, into your soul. I'll make you a heroine, a Madonna, a Messalina, by turns, and you'll only emerge from the purple of palaces to walk in the azure of paradise . . ."

"You're an eccentric, and that's why I love you."

"You love me, so allow yourself to be guided by me. I know magic waters that metamorphose those who plunge into them. I want to take you there, Edwige. Lean on me, close your eyes, forget that you're alive, forget that you're thinking, allow yourself to be enveloped by my embrace, penetrated by the effluvia of my dreams, abducted into the beyond that I divine and where I want to travel with you. Stick your lips to my lips, let me plunge my eyes into your mauve eyes; don't speak any more, don't think any more, don't dream any more. Do I not have dreams enough for two?"

"Alas," she said, "can a dream be shared? Are you not going to become an egotistic musician for whom I shall be an insensible lyre? You imagine that the lyre that serves to procure you exquisite sensations will feel them and share them, but is that really true?"

"Don't say that, Edwige, souls can penetrate one another; it's sufficient that one of them consents to it and abandons itself, but it's necessary that it abandons itself truly and entirely. Do you want to attempt that, Edwige?"

"I'd like to try."

※

For the first time—after innumerable supplications!—Edwige has consented to come home with me.

For hours on end we have talked, in low voices, eyes gazing into eyes and lips close to lips, and it is evening, evening already, and for fear of falling back, at the end of those delectable hours, into the banal hubbub of the streets, and in order not to interrupt this day of felicity, Edwige will not go away . . .

And already, near the alcove, with emotional gestures, I help her to undress, while she babbles about frivolous things.

"Don't you share my opinion? I like tight bodices and narrow skirts, simple garments without frills. I generally choose fabrics with bright but discreet shades, a little dark; I detest variegation and garish colors. Don't you agree? Yes, I can see that that astonishes you slightly. In spite of the fashion that wants black or assorted colors in attire, I wear white stockings, white stockings like those women wore twenty years ago. What do you expect? It's a mania; when I was young, Maman only gave me those, and since then, I've never been able to decide to have others. However, if it irritates you . . ."

"No, Edwige, what do these frivolous details matter?"

"Well, it's like colored lingerie. Today, all women have chemises of black, blue, yellow or red surah . . . I find that horrible. You'll only ever see me in chemises of white batiste, but of an extreme delicacy, with expensive lace. Don't you think that's in better taste than all their black, blue or red surahs?"

"I agree with you, Edwige."

"I still admit colored silks for skirts, but for the rest, no. As for bloomers, I never wear them. That's another old habit, a mania, if you like; Maman never wore any. She brought me up not to wear them, and I couldn't decide to put them on. however, if you desire . . ."

"Why would I ask you to multiply the obstacles between your flesh and mine?"

"In any case, personally, I'm for simplifying my costume as much as possible . . . I don't like long and complicated undressings. So, you see, you'll very rarely see me in a corset; I have a rather slim waist, and sufficiently shapely to do without one, and I don't see why I should impose a torture on myself . . . am I boring you?"

"Edwige, please shut up. What do the garments you wear, and those you don't want to wear, matter? Am I not going to take you away to fabulous lands where I can dress you with my own hands in sumptuous costumes of which you can't dream? Oh, if it pleases me to take you to Watteau's Cythera, will you not be able to keep under your pigeon-throat panel dresses your dear white stockings and fine batiste chemises? And if it pleases me to metamorphose you into a goddess of ancient Olympus, will you think about putting under your candid linen tunic a silk skirt, a corset or bloomers? So don't worry, no one will contradict what you call your little manias but please, shut up, shut up! Stick your mouth to my mouth and let yourself be carried away into the dreams that will please me."

"That's true," she said. "I'd forgotten our pact."

✷

On what river of dreams are we embarked? Toward what impossible land, florid with the flowers of dream, are we sailing on this silver boat with sails of white satin?

Do we know? And why should we know? Is it not sufficient for us to know that the water is the color of sapphire, that the sky is exquisitely roseate, that the banks between which we are gliding are full of palm trees, laburnums, oleanders and miraculous efflorescences?

Ibises and flamingoes pass overhead, and little song-birds come to flutter around our sail, chirping. Butterflies as beautiful as enamels sway in the air and sometimes come to settle on Edwige's mouth, which they mistake for a rose.

We are both sitting in the prow of the boat, and we allow our bare feet to dangle, tickled by the crests of the waves.

I have taken Edwige's fingers in my hand and she has stuck her lips to my lips, and the gentle rocking of the boat, and the heady effluvia of the flowers, and the perfumed breath of the breeze, and the murmur of the waves and the warmth of the sky all intoxicate us, and our bodies are tipped back on the crimson cushions, and,

35

our bare feet dangling over the water for hours on end, we felt very slow and ineffable felicities flowing, sinking into abysms of happiness, and sometimes the sensation of sinking into a voluptuous ocean became so paradisal, became so sharp, that our respiration became halting, and little cries escaped us, and our two hearts froze and we thought we were dying . . .

"Daylight already," said Edwige. "Oh, it's too much, my beloved. Let's sleep . . ."

"Edwige! Oh, why did you speak?"

"That's true . . . I'd forgotten our agreement."

It is in a fabulous décor of old. The thousand spires of fantastic cathedrals, the gables, the dentellate pinnacles, the statues of Gothic houses and the black towers of belfries puncture the azure. It is like an inextricable stone vegetation in the sky, from which frightful grimacing gargoyles protrude everywhere, mouths open, necks extended, like serpents with the heads of ghouls or unicorns. All the walls and all the porches are sculpted like jewels. Naively painted Madonnas are dreaming in ogival niches; Christs are agonizing among the foliage and heraldic beasts of columns; on the roofs, forests of saints are holding up their aureoled heads; monks, dwarfs and madmen are grimacing on the cornices and the architraves, and along the friezes, angels are sounding the trumpets of the last judgment; the dead are resuscitating, the just going to the right of God among the choirs of cherubim; hideous devils with gaping jaws are dragging the howling damned into the infernal boat, while the sun makes the crimsons, emeralds, azures and sinoples of stained glass rutilant everywhere.

"Edwige, don't you want to walk with me among these architectures of dream?"

As they pass before the holy sculptures, the men uncover their heads and pray, the women kneel down . . .

Oh, the poverty is great and bellies are often empty. But does anyone have the time to think about poverty and bellies that are crying famine? A mystical wind is blowing through the realm. It is not bodies that are wandering through the streets, but souls, and there is certainly no poverty for souls and no famine for souls. Oh, how they find on all sides, those pure, ingenuous souls, the bread that satisfies them. Oh, the fine feast, eternally served for them: it is the prayer of the architecture, which rises toward the azure; it is the prayer of the bells that soars in the azure; it is the prayer of the organs, which flies toward the azure; it is the prayer of the stone Christs and Madonnas; it is the prayer of the orisons that escape from the windows of convents.

Life is hard and evil, to be sure, but one does not live in life; one lives in the hope of blue beyonds where cherubim with golden harps flutter. What do the miseries of this life matter, which is only a temporary encampment? Oh, it is only to add a little charm to the rude hours of initiation that anyone takes the trouble to embellish them by sculpting in stone, immobilizing in the colors of the stained glass windows and frescoes those marvelous dreams of paradise.

And then, as soon as that vain but immortal task is accomplished, without concern for corporeal enjoyments, one hastens toward the mysterious door of death, and it is not despair and terror, it is the joy of deliverance, the joy that degenerates into a mad bacchanal. Hup! Hup! It is the fair of death, the tambours and the rebecs play crazy, vertiginous reels, it is the epilepsy of the *danse macabre*, festive skeletons dancing jigs, and now, drunk, arrogant with gaiety, laughing to rip their shrouds, clerics, barons, vagrants, whores and damsels whirl around benevolent Death, around the concierge of Heaven.

"Good Reaper, deliver us! Deliver us from this death that is life, rid us of these rags that are our flesh and let us fly into eternal life! Good Reaper, let us pass . . . are we not worthy to soar among the divine phalanges? Why should we dread the balance that will weigh our souls? Have we not, thwarting the ruses of the Evil One, spat on the illusory pleasures of down here; have we not incarcerated in cloisters the shame of our bodies, have we not combated the miscreants; have we not lived in the hope of the immortal life; have we not—the supreme virtue— spent our time putting our holy dreams into songs, painting them on walls, and sculpting them in stone? So, good Reaper, see, now that you are opening your good door to us, we are joyful, like captives being set free. Joy is making our hearts overflow. A wind of delirium is blowing over us and intoxicating us. Let's go! Hup! Hup! Faster, tambours and rebecs! Let's dance, let's whirl, let's dance like lunatics!

"And let us dance too, and let us laugh like lunatics too, we who have not been able to thwart the ruses of the Evil One, we who are awaiting the eternal tortures of Hell. We have read the forbidden grimoires, we have copulated with the goat of the Sabbat, we have spat on the host and soiled the sacred pyx with our urine. In order to be the masters of black sciences we have sold our souls to the Devil, and now that the hour of payment is about to sound, we are arriving, joyfully, as honest debtors, to acquit our debt. Open the door to us, good Reaper, rid us of the hideous mantle of our body. Oh, we know that the grimacing demons are lying in wait for us; they will drag us away and roll us into the frightful gulf of inextinguishable fire. But what does it matter? The thirst to savor that terrible unknown is devouring us; we want to know, we want to know . . . and then, we have been trailing our odious carnal rags long enough, and now that we sense that you want to rid us of them, good Reaper, joy is making our hearts overflow. A wind of delirium is blowing over us and intoxicating us. Let's go! Hup! Hup! Faster, tambours and rebecs! Let's dance, let's whirl, let's dance like lunatics . . . !

"Don't you want, Edwige, don't you want to walk with me amid these architectures of dream, to walk with these souls that are wandering amid these architectures of dream . . . ?"

Here comes the crowd that is running from all the streets into the main square of the city. The belfry is ringing joyfully, the trumpets clamoring, sparkling banners floating in the air. On balconies of wrought iron or stone, perforated like floating lace, at windows, at skylights, on the ledges of gables, people are pressing and gazing. Hacks, palfreys, white mules with crimson caparisons and snorting chargers are cleaving through the people, who bow down before the rutilant brocade skirts of ladies in high hennins, the ugly mugs of mitered priests and the golden armor of barons. On the steps of the square, decked with watered silk, the brocaded silk dresses and damascenes armor are shining. The squires are galloping to make the rabble and the servants line up. The herald of arms has blown his tuba three times, and here comes the young and beautiful Bradamante, mounted on a hippogriff that twirls in the air, who advances, her lance menacing, to encounter the black knight whose charger is snorting grimly and prancing in the arena . . .

"Edwige, let's go closer and watch this heroic armed combat. Let's mingle with the crowd of these noble spectators. Perhaps some brave knight errant will recount his distant and crazy adventures to us, his rides through the enchanted forest, his battles against giants and griffins, the evil spells of the enchanter Merlin. Perhaps he will tell us about the paladin Roland, Lancelot, Arthur and the sons of Aymon, and Ogier of the Lake . . . Doubtless he will tell us about the bravery of the knights of the Round Table, and the conquest of the Holy Grail, and how he saw the blonde Angelique carried away into the air, stark naked, on the rump of the flying beast . . .

"Or, if you prefer, let's draw away. And now, mingled with this crowd of the common people who are listening religiously to that troubadour stationed near the signpost of the crossroads, we too can lend an ear to his tender chant, accompanied by his monotonous rebec. Listen, is he not singing the glorious adventures of Blancheflor, the meek, impossibly beautiful virgin who became the wife of the Emperor Pepin . . . ?

When Blancheflor arrived in Paris
Richly clad with Duke Aubris,
Hair scattered, in a mousy coat,
The palfrey on which she was seated
Was whiter than a lily flower.
Her waist was slender, her eyes lovely,
Her mouth firm with little teeth
Brighter than that polished ivory,
Her hips low and calves taut,
Neatly held in pricy stockings,
Feet well shod and forehead silvery,
Pert breasts and arched eyebrows.
Thus, more beautiful than had ever been seen,
That virgin on entering Paris,
Falling in long waves over her white neck,
Her blonde hair, from which a little chaplet
Of gold and onyx discreetly emerged.
All the streets filled up in Paris,
And immediately everyone said:
"How pretty that lady is!
She ought to hold a kingdom!
Please God that the Emperor takes her
For a wife! Oh, let us all beware
Of the imperium of those eyes!

"Ah! The bells! The air is full of the sound of bells, the joyful sound of bells. The bass notes of the cathedral are rumbling, the carillons of a thousand granite bell-towers are trilling, dingdonging, tintinnabulating . . . ! Here are the vespers, Edwige . . . here are the vespers ringing . . . !"

Edwige was sitting, half naked on the bed, and I dressed her, as one does a small child, but with gestures of pious caress, and as I came devotedly to knot her ribboned garter at her knee, from which long azure curls floated over the dazzling whiteness of her stocking, she said to me:

"But all that, all that we just saw and heard, was it not, in hours long since vanished, a present, a material and brutal present like the one from which you want to flee far away?"

"Undoubtedly. But what does it matter to us? The present isn't wounding and ugly by virtue of its materiality. As soon as it has passed via the waters of memory, its materiality is dissolved and nothing any longer remains of it but the eternally beautiful thought. Isn't the past, Edwige, the only thing really existent? Isn't the present only the incubation of the idea in the egg? It's necessary that it breaks the shell of present materiality in order to fly away into the sky. The only thing that truly exists is the past . . ."

"Do you want us to live exclusively in memory, then?"

"That is more truly living than living exclusively in the present. But be patient, Edwige; I will show you, in a world of dream, what will no longer appear to you as memory . . . and yet, will it not also be? Are we doing anything, when we think that we are inventing the most fabulous chimeras, other than evoking visions, unconsciously remembered, of times when our souls relaxed in the marvelous Eden of Pure Ideas?"

"Could we not return there, to that Eden?"

"Perhaps."

"Oh, that would be nice!"

Now standing in front of the mirror, Edwige made her pallor paler with a powder-puff of rice-powder.

✳

In that rural region there was an old shady and little-used road, an old road so little-used that at a certain place, at the edge of a little wood, the ground was covered with thick grass, beautiful moss, daisies and buttercups.

Edwige and I had chosen that pretty deserted spot in order to roll our idleness and our dreams there on warm summer afternoons, amid the thick grass, the beautiful moss, the daisies and the buttercups. Swarms of little butterflies of all colors were fluttering around us incessantly, and the air was full of the chirping of sparrows and the trills of warblers.

But one day, we saw a man appear in our pretty little desert, richly clad in black, followed by a crew of laborers with muddy blouses.

The man in black, with great cruel and indignant gestures, showed his fist to the grass, the moss, the daisies and the buttercups, and on his order, the crew of laborers, with spades and pickaxes, charged upon the beautiful carpet of flowers and verdure.

Edwige and I threw ourselves at the feet of the man in black, weeping and imploring mercy for our beautiful moss, daisies and buttercups.

"Let's go, let's go!" yapped the pitiless executioner. "Am I not the engineer of bridges and highways?"

The engineer Bildebières, to whom I related that event, said that I was wrong.

"The beauty of a road," he told me, "cannot, in any case—you hear me, in any case,—result from its poor maintenance. Besides which, you'll certainly admit that an engineer of bridges and highways must have a certain competence relative to this question, since he has spent his life studying these problems, to which you, as well as Madame, are complete strangers?"

"But," I said, "the little birds that love that moss and those flowers will no longer come to sing in that corner devastated by spades and pickaxes."

"What a pity!" interrupted the engineer; and, folding his arms over his breast, he cried: "Then you, too, are amused by birds that sing? I'll permit myself once again, my dear, not to share your opinion. I don't know anything in the world more hair-raising than the shriek of a bird . . . *pipipicouicouicouipipipi* . . . it gets on my nerves, it drives me mad. So, listen, at my country house, wasn't there a dirty nightingale that had the idea on installing itself in a wood in my park, right next to the house? All night long there were whistlings to shatter your eardrums, to drive you mad . . . no means of closing an eye for a minute. I was foaming at the mouth, I was in a state of indescribable rage.

"Finally, one night, I couldn't stand it any longer; I leapt out of bed, I took my rifle, and without getting dressed, in trousers and a nightcap, I went down to lie

in ambush in my park . . . oh, it was a long and difficult
hunt; the night was dark, and then, a nightingale isn't
very big, and it hides adroitly in the foliage, and then,
finally, it's necessary to admit it, I'm not a marvelous
shot. Again and again, I thought I saw it, and then, *bang!*
bang! I fired both barrels, and immediately, behind me, I
heard a whistle mocking me. I turned round furiously,
bang! bang! to the right, *bang! bang!* to the left, *bang! bang!*
up above, down below, in front of me, behind me, *bang!*
bang! bang! bang!

"There was a terrible interminable nocturnal fusil-
lade. The house woke up; all the windows lit up and
opened. The white forms of men and women leaned
out. Anxious faces interrogated, sounded the thickets of
the park, convinced that the château was under attack
from hundreds of brigands. But that was all the same
to me; I was mad, intoxicated by the powder, rendered
furious by that hair-raising whistling fluttering from tree
to tree. *Bang! bang! bang!* I fired in all directions without
aiming, without stopping . . .

"The doors of the château opened, my guests came
down, barely dressed, armed with rifles themselves. The
people of the village had come running in alarm; they'd
climbed over the wall and were advancing cautiously,
their weapons ready. *Bang! bang!* I was still firing. I had
been recognized. They asked me what I wanted them to
do, 'Shoot, then! Shoot!' I shouted at them.

"'Where? At what?' The question came from all sides.

"'At the nightingale! At the nightingale!'

"Then, it was frightful. Shots departed from everywhere at the same time. A nourished, uninterrupted fusil-

lade commenced. *Bang! bang! bang! bang!* One couldn't hear any longer, the air was full of smoke, the lead whistled, tree branches and leaves rained down, cut to shreds. That lasted until daylight. For a long time, already, the accursed nightingale could no longer be heard twittering.

"Finally, when the sun had risen, searching carefully on the ground literally covered with cartridge-cases and foliage riddled by lead shot and the cadavers of little birds, we ended up finding a little creature, all gray and horribly ugly. It was him! Even though he was dead, I crushed him under my heel!"

In the solitary garden of the guinguette with green tables, Edwige was sitting on the swing and swinging gently while talking to me.

Because of the heat she had unfastened her bodice and undone her hair. I could perceive a little of the pale flesh of her meager cleavage, and I followed with my eyes the floating of her light hair, which was fluttering in accordance with the rhythm of the swing, like fine threads of golden silk, almost silver in color. Sometimes, at the hazard of the oscillations, her skirt was lifted up, and I glimpsed her slim legs with aristocratic ankles, modeled in those unfashionable white stockings of which she was so proud, and my gaze ran from her flying hair to her naked cleavage, from the beribboned steel buckle of her little pumps to the mauve flower of her eyes.

"Have you retained the desire, Edwige," I asked her, "for the vulgar amour of other men, and do you still think that we're burying ours too much under gems and flowers?"

I shivered with joy when she replied:

"In truth, I thought that for some time, and I loved more in curiosity than conviction the sumptuous and unprecedented ruses of your kisses, and I followed you into the countries you showed me rather like an actress playing without conviction the role of tourist in landscapes that she knows only too well to be painted scenery . . . but truly, I'm beginning to get used to these new lands and to love them without doubting their existence. I truly feel that an imperious and gentle soul, which is yours, has gradually penetrated mine, and that my soul has abdicated omnipotence, and is no longer commanding my actions, my ideas or my words. In any case, yesterday, I understood definitively, in listening to the engineer Bildebières, that it is necessary that there *really exists* another world than the one in which the killers of nightingales put on a semblance of living, and I understood quite clearly that in taking me by the hand you have led me far from the world of appearances, into the sky of verities."

"That's right," I said to her. "Ugliness evidently cannot have a real existence. It is negative in essence. The world in which one kills nightingales cannot really exist, and we ought to feel sorry for those who lapse into that stupid illusion."

"But what troubles me," Edwige interjected, "is that your amour for me isn't without some scorn, since my being doesn't matter very much and you have the power to recreate it perpetually . . ."

"Does your being exist more than the rest? Isn't it sufficient for you that I love the idea of which it is only the imperfect sign? What does it matter that you are sacrificing to me a ridiculous pride, if, at that price, I am guiding you to happiness? And besides, Edwige, remember that your soul, the abdication of which you still seem to be mourning somewhat, which you thought to be integrally itself yesterday, was undoubtedly not itself, and that yours has only truly existed since it has encountered the other soul, mine, of which its light was only a fragment detached an eternity ago, and which, for an eternity, has tended to come and confound itself in the lost unity. So have no more scruples, and resign yourself to no longer being anything but mine."

"It's necessary, it's very necessary that I resign myself to that sacrifice of no longer being anything but one of your thoughts, a slave of your fantasies, of no longer being anything but you, for I sense now that I would weep eternally if I went back to the world in which people shoot nightingales."

"In this *fête galante* park, Boucher's chubby little amours are fluttering around the swing. The boscage is full of the sighs of amorous marquises, and while you're swinging, Edwige, I'm dreaming an exquisitely-wrought madrigal in which I shall call you Phyllis."

In what land of fable was I walking with Edwige?

I recall that there were monumental palaces, the walls of which were constructed of gold, silver and enameled bricks, in which monsters and gods were immobilized. Granite statues laden with jewelry and sumptuous decorations were erected on all sides. Amid crazy vegetation, jets of perfumed water sobbed into immense basins of sardonyx. The vapors of a thousand cassolettes rose vertically into a sky of a blue purer than sapphire.

On an immense peristyle shaded by rich awnings of multicolored fabrics, amid crimson carpets and cushion, tiger skins and the debris of a fine feast, clad in the royal robe and tiara, rutilant with gems, the monarch of these strange kingdoms was enthroned, dead drunk, his beard stained by wine. At his feet, disheveled women swarmed. Some, completely naked, as white as ivory statues or as red as statues of polished bronze, were arching their bodies in lustful poses; others, half-dressed in gauzes as transparent as glass, were rolling on the ground, finishing drinking scented wine from amphorae, interlacing their limbs, laughing and singing; others, finally, in order to reawaken the desires of the royal and magnificent drunkard, were dancing before him to the rhythm of a barbaric and lascivious music; from time to time they lifted up their hyacinth robes, with the slow and hieratic gestures of priestesses, uncovering to the indifferent eyes of their master the scintillating nudity of their beautiful thighs and their depilated abdomens . . .

Young black slaves were agitating immense fans made of peacock feathers around the torpid monarch . . .

I contemplated that rare and magnificent spectacle with Edwige, with my dear Edwige, and we were getting drunk on the precious perfumes, the aphrodisiac perfumes that were floated in the air, when a voice, which did not resemble the voices of the inhabitants of that singular realm, made us shudder by calling us by our names

"Hey! Monsieur Hans! Madame Edwige!"

We turned round. It was the engineer Bildebières.

"Aha! You were on the Moon again, my good lunatics!" he said, with a gross smile, grabbing me by a button. "Is it so very amusing, then, walking on the Moon?"

"Certainly," I replied. "More amusing than walking on the bitumen of your boulevards."

"I don't share your opinion. There's nothing as interesting as the great roads of a modern capital. All that mad activity, that fever of labor, that contention of all the wills of a crowd swarming toward the production of the useful, seems to me to be a sublime spectacle, and I'm astonished that you, a poet, have never thought of writing anything in verse about that, I don't like verses, as you know, but after all, if poets acquired the habit of treating serious subjects, it would be better than nothing; they'd be less insupportable and one would be able to tolerate them, especially if they consented to treat those serious subjects, not in verse, but in good prose, very simple, very clear, very precise . . .

"So, look, the signs, the posters, they never suggest anything to you? Well, personally, if I wrote, I'd write something marvelous about signs. What a superb subject! The struggle for existence by means of simple colored letters, the robbery of passers-by by means of simple vocables! Oh, the sign, that's the true literature of the coming century. Look, you have nothing to do, let's go up to the top deck of this tram, let's go amuse ourselves reading them. You'll see whether you know a more marvelous, more ingenious poem . . ."

We were obliged to accompany the engineer Bildebières to his top deck, and make a semblance of waxing ecstatic with him.

So, now my head is full of ridiculous words written in golden, silver, blue, red, white, black and yellow letters, which are dancing dolorously in my head:

TEETH AND DENTURES FILLED

CURE OF SECRET MALADIES WITHOUT
MERCURY OR DANGER OF RELAPSE

FRANCO-RUSSIAN EAU DE COLOGNE

English Tailor
Riding costumes made to measure
or for hire
Trousers for horses

Specialty of syphonic bidets

IF YOU HAVE A HEADACHE
BUY AN AERO-TRANSPARENT HAT
IF YOU DON'T HAVE ONE
BUY ONE IN ORDER TO AVOID THEM

WHITE PETROL
ABSOLUTELY UNINFLAMMABLE

KOREAN DYNAMITE

INFALLIBLE LOTION FOR HAIR-LOSS

STEAM LABORATORY

PURCHASE AND SALE OF PAWN-TICKETS

AT THE SIGN OF THE KINGFISHER
HUNTING AND FISHING APPARATUS
CARP LIQUOR, FIVE FRANCS A BOTTLE

MOURNING DRESS IN 24 HOURS

HYGIENIC COFFINS ENTIRELY IN GLASS

Oh, will we ever be able, now, Edwige, to return to that beautiful land of fable where we saw, in a monumental palace with walls constructed of gold, silver and enamel bricks, that strange dead-drunk monarch, amid flowers, crimson carpets and naked women?

"Look in there, Edwige."

The heads and hearts are swarming in the same dream. The heads and hearts are floating in the same vat of blood and flesh. The hearts are stroking one another, the heads colliding. The hearts are kissing one another, the heads are biting one another. And all of them, the heads and hearts, are floating and swarming in the same vat of blood and flesh. And yet those hearts and those heads are so dissimilar that one can scarcely apply the terms *hearts* and *heads* to them, however generously . . .

And now, in the vat of blood and flesh, amid the confusion of hearts and heads, a laureate head has loomed up, and a heart crowned with brambles has loomed up, and the laureate head and the heart crowned with thorns have cried: "We are dreaming of chimeras that none of these bloody heads suspects: Lord, why then are we plunged in this vat of blood and flesh, among all these swarming heads and hearts?"

"Look in there, Edwige, look into that bloody vat."

"Uh oh!" said the engineer Bildebières."Uh oh! Don't you have a malady of the will?"

"A malady of the . . . ?"

"Of the will, exactly. Of the will. It's very frequent today. Look, out of every ten people passing by in the street, at least seven . . ."

"Truly?"

"Exactly . . . and those seven people don't suspect it. They're like you, they don't suspect it, absolutely not! That's what explains the decadence into which our unfortunate fatherland is sinking . . . the wind of demoralization that is blowing over us . . . the truly alienated who, under the pretext of art, of poetry . . . But don't worry, that malady can be cured. Although our century is swarming with madmen and utopians, fortunately, it can also glorify itself in being the century of science. Paris doesn't only have those idlers who, under the pretext of smearing paper with colors or rhymes . . . there are also

true savants whose works are, I believe, more beautiful
and more useful . . . Doctor Cocon,[1] for example. He has
made a specialty of intellectual pathology; he's one of
the princes of science. Of, if all these wretched bohemi-
ans who encumber the city would consent to be treated
by him, how quickly he would cure the disease of poetry
and the fever of the ideal from which they're suffering!
How quickly he would return them to productive society!
How quickly he would change them, for their own good
and the good of society, into productive individuals, into
scientists, into engineers, into pharmacists! Oh, believe
me, go and see Doctor Cocon; he'll cure you of your
horrible malady."

I have followed the advice of the engineer Bildebières,
and have come to see Doctor Cocon.

After waiting for two hours in a luxurious drawing
room hung with simulated Oriental drapes, a uniformed
valet introduces me into the consulting-room of the
prince of science.

The room is simultaneously rich, sober and severe. It
has plum-colored wallpaper and there are bronzes on all
the items of furniture, which are called art.

The prince is standing behind his work-table. He is
vaguely reminiscent of a sixty-year-old Napoléon I in a
black frock coat.

____

1 The French *cocon* is the equivalent of the English word cocoon,
but one cannot help suspecting that the author also has in mind the
similar term *cochon* [pig].

As soon as I begin to speak he interrupts me, brutally and peremptorily.

"No need, Monsieur, no need! I know . . . I can see what the problem is."

"But . . ."

"You have a malady of the will . . . that's it . . . caused by a hypertrophy of the imagination."

"Oh! Damn . . . !" I said, anxiously.

"It's serious, in fact," he went on, "but have no fear; I've cured many others."

He took steel forceps and long silver needles from a medical bag, which he scattered on the plum-colored table-top.

"Yes," he went on, "I'll cure you. It's quite simple. I'll begin by trepanning you . . ."

"By . . . ?"

"Yes, by opening your skull."

"Permit me . . ."

"I shall open your skull, Monsieur. It's a delicate operation, of course, but not dangerous. So, I'll open your skull, and then, once your skull is open, with these silver pins you can see, I'll puncture your dreams, one by one . . ."

"What, Doctor? You'll puncture my dreams?"

"Exactly."

"But what will remain of me then?"

"You'll still have your logical, positive intelligence, the marvelous faculty that you lack, but which distinguishes humans from animals: Reason."

"Oh, but Doctor, life without dreams! Life without dreams! That's terrible . . ."

Doctor Cocon shrugged his shoulders.

"You'll become similar to serious people, sane people—the engineer Bildebières, for example . . ."

It was no longer Doctor Cocon who was talking to me, it was no longer his rich, sober and severe consulting-room, with its plum-colored wallpaper and bronzes called art on all the items of furniture.

I found myself in a flowery Eden, at the foot of the palm-tree of Science. I was—yes, I remember it—I was Eve, and the Evil One, in the form of a serpent with the head of Aesculapius, crawled toward me, and said to me, seductively:

"If you want, you'll be similar to the engineer Bildebières. You'll be similar to the engineer Bildebières . . ."

Then, suddenly, I remembered the archangel with the flaming sword expelling the sinners from the flowery Eden and precipitating them into the gulf of labor and dolor, and, showing a hateful fist to the reptilian tempter, I cried:

"No, get back, subtle serpent! Back, Satan! Satan who wants to steal the paradise of my dreams from me now! I won't let you pierce the ovaries of my dreams with your forked and sterilizing tongue. Back, Satan!"

And I fled, while Doctor Cocon gurgled: "Poor boy! Poor crackpot!"

In the bedroom, faintly lit by a mauve crystal night-light, Edwige and I, by virtue of a sentiment of profound modesty that commanded us to avoid the vulgar indecency of the transparent attire of the alcove, had stripped naked, chastely naked.

She was sitting on the bed, braiding her long pale gold hair, and as I was contemplating her elegant and slender forms, which seemed not so much those of a woman as of a young ephebe, she said to me: "Why isn't this room an Eden guarded by the cherub with the flaming sword? We could walk amid the fabulous flowers. I would be Eve and you would be Adam . . . for we're as scantily clad as they were."

"You know, Edwige, that the cherub with the flaming sword expelled our ancestors and all their descendants from Eden."

"However, didn't you promise me, once, to take me to that Eden, into that garden where the pure ideas flourish?"

"Certainly, for a redemption exists—a redemption for those who are able to detach themselves from things of the earth and the desire for false knowledge that doomed Eve. Those have the right to fly back to the fabulous garden, and when they return among humans they cannot help singing the praises of the marvels they have contemplated, and what they sing is so prodigiously beautiful, and their tone is so sublime, that people mock them and stone them."

As caressant as a beautiful serpent, Edwige came to coil her supple body around mine, and murmured into my lips: "Let's go, then, for I no longer fear the mockery or the stones of men."

✳

57

In the inn by the roadside there was a large stable with golden mangers, and it was not horses that were pawing the ground impatiently in that strange stable, but unicorns and chimeras.

When we had chosen the mount that suited us from among those legendary beasts, a young groom, a handsome as a page, led it to the door of the inn for us. It was a gigantic unicorn with a red coat; smoke and flame escaped from its nostrils. It tore the ground impatiently with its claws, and its immense wings were quivering with the desire for flight.

On the side of the road there were people who gazed at us with stupid eyes, and who spat insults at us. Children even threw little stones at us, and one obese woman, dressed in green silk, laughed with so much force that her fat belly, which she tried to master with both hands, leapt and rolled, as if she had angry cats under her skirts. A legless cripple threatened us with fists enclosed in heavy shoes, and prostitutes insulted us with obscene gestures.

In order to flee that ignoble crowd, we decided to hasten our departure. I leapt on to the back of the flying beast, and Edwige, aided by the young groom as handsome as a page, who made a stirrup for her with his two hands, soon set herself astride it behind me; and, the unicorn having pointed the spike on its forehead toward the sun and deployed its immense wings, we were in the sky, far from the stupid insults of the crowd.

※

We had tethered the unicorn to a tree-trunk, and we had penetrated into the marvelous garden.

Troubling odors were exhaled from the trees in flower, and a light and perfumed mist refreshed our temples, without making the smallest leaf tremble.

As we were wandering in the marvelously beautiful garden, Edwige said to me: "That's strange; we're walking in this marvelous garden, and yet I sense that we're not walking, that our legs aren't moving."

"We no longer have any legs, Edwige. We no longer have any bodies; we're in the garden of truth, and the appearance that was our flesh has vanished; we're ourselves now."

"Oh! It's very singular! We're walking in this mysterious garden, and our gazes are ecstatic in contemplating all the admirable flowers, and yet I certainly wouldn't be able to say whether it's as immense as infinite space or whether it occupies no space at all in the world."

"Doubtless, Edwige, there is no space any longer, and space was only an illusory appearance that has evaporated, in the fires of that beautiful sun motionless in that azure."

"Hans! Have we been in this marvelous garden for a long time? I truly don't know how long we've been in this marvelous garden."

"There is no time any more, Edwige; there's no more time, and everything here simply is, and can't become, nor have been. There's no time any more."

"Tell me, Hans, why these flowers and these leaves aren't moving, why we aren't moving, why nothing is moving in this marvelous garden."

"Because everything is beautiful here with the supreme beauty, and the slightest movement would break the absolute harmony necessary to that supreme beauty."

"Hans, I feel lighter than a perfume and you appear to me to be as beautiful as the gleam of precious stones, as beautiful as the marvelous motionless flowers that surround us, and I'm happy, with a happiness that I'd be afraid to express in human words."

"Try, though."

"It's a voluptuousness that is sharp and soft at the same time, of which one thinks one is going to die, and which never ends and doesn't diminish. You won't be jealous of what I'm going to say?"

"No."

"Well, it's as if I were lying with God, and by hugging my unworthy body in his arms he's communicating the indescribable frisson that will secure my marrows the gift of eternity."

"That's it, Edwige. Such is the voluptuousness that is embracing us."

"But please, what is this mysterious garden? In what corner of the world is it located?"

"This mysterious garden, Edwige, is Eden, and Eden is the world . . . and doubtless we haven't changed location. But today, we've seen the splendid truth through the ugly everyday illusions."

✳

The engineer Bildebières held Doctor Cocon in the highest esteem, en entirely sublime esteem that he usually reserved for mortals who had graduated from the École Polytechnique. Madame Bildebières liked to receive him and entertain him, even though he only talked willingly about anatomy, pathology and very specialized matters, with redoubtable technical terms that made the head ache. When he entered the drawing room, with his overly long black coat and his disquieting Napoleonic physiognomy, all conversation died away and the ladies—all the ladies—darted slightly bright gazes toward him: interested, almost admiring gazes; the kind of gazes that women are accustomed to direct at heroes rather than scientists.

That was because a mysterious legend floated over the life of Doctor Cocon.

He had an enormous scar on his right hand. His thumb and two of his fingers seemed denuded of flesh, no longer having anything but skin over the bone; and it was whispered that it had a tenebrous history, the story of a bloody drama of which not all the details were known, except to the two actors, who had been Doctor Cocon and a lion . . .

A lion! That had been enough to go to the heads of all the ladies who frequented Madame Bildebières' house. Doctor Cocon had appeared to them as a bold tamer of wild beasts, having had adorably frightening adventures in his life; and they liked to imagine him out there, in the tropical latitudes, lying in ambush, his rifle shouldered, among palm trees, cacti and roars, waiting by night for the terrible bound of the carnivores, felling them with a bullet in the heart, or, knife in hand, fighting at close quarters with tigers, lions or panthers.

Relative to those terrible events, doubtless accomplished in his youth, he maintained an absolute discretion. When anyone attempted to lead the conversation to that topic, he had a fashion of coughing distractedly and saying, with a malign smile: "Oh! Oh . . . lions! Lions . . . !"

And then, without adding another word on that subject, to the great despair of the anxious ladies, he contrived to turn the conversation away, to talk about his pamphlet entitled: *Poetry Considered as an Inflammatory and Heredtiary Affection of Certain Tissues in the Fissure of Rolando, its Diagnosis, its Etiology and its Treatment.* Or he began to sing the praises of the report that his friend Léocade Lendormy had presented to the Acdémie des Inscriptions on the subject of *Analogies and Differences between the institution of the Praetura among the Romans and that of the modern Mont-de-Piété.*[1] Or he started to summarize for those distracted ladies a fine book by his other friend Gatien Leputois, entitled: *Egyptian Mummies Considered as Alimentary Conserves,* in which the latter demonstrated definitively that the ancient Egyptians were anthropophages and that mummies served as nourishment for their armies in the course of distant expeditions.

All that, evidently, although very interesting, only satisfied the ladies in part, but had for its ultimate result

1 This is a joke, Roman praetors being magistrates of a sort, while the Mont-de-Piété functioned in Paris as a kind of pawnbroker lending small amounts of money at interest on the security of pledged goods; the French *prête*r, to lend, does come from the same Latin root as praetor, signifying "beyond," but the course of the etymological derivation is not obvious in either case.

that of sharpening their curiosity further, making their imagination work harder and augmenting, if possible, their admiration for the doctor, who combined such modest discretion with the bravery and heroism that he was divined to have.

If anyone persisted in trying to lead the conversation to exotic countries, with the hope that the doctor might be induced, by an association of ideas, to talk about his hunts, he limited himself very skillfully to giving the conversation an exclusively scientific direction, commencing with his customary eloquence some discourse on a subject in ethnography, anthropology or botany.

"Oh, Africa, Africa!" he might say, for example. "Africa, the land of palm trees! Well, Mesdames, with regard to palm trees, one thing that perhaps you don't know is that those trees do not only grow in the tropical latitudes. One very interesting variety exists that grows under our gray and inclement sky. I was the first to study it; I discovered it. You may refer to the long treatise I wrote on the subject ten years ago: *Monograph on Palma nigra*. Yes, Mesdames, *Palma nigra coconis*, the black palm, for the palm is black, entirely black, black in the bark and black in the foliage. Unlike the other species of the palm genus, it seems to be fond of damp places, such as river banks. It is also extremely rare. In spite of my research, I have only been able to observe a single specimen, and you'll never guess where. In the middle of Paris, a few steps from the Pont Neuf. It seems to have taken root in the very bed of the Seine, for its elegant and graceful stem traverses the boat of floating baths named the

Samaritaine,[1] and launches through the roof, which is thus gracefully and naturally crowned by an elegant dome of the most beautiful black foliage. Unfortunately, I have not been able to take the study of that curious vegetal species further because of the hostility of the owner of the bathing establishment."

And the ladies had to bear the expense of their ruses yet again.

I had observed for some time that Edwige herself, who had witnessed several of those conversations, was beginning to share the curiosity of the ladies, and even to manifest a certain admiration for the mysterious doctor, the discreet hero. Ordinarily so passive in being entirely mine, to the point of no longer thinking, dreaming, acting or talking about anything but me, for some days she had been making attempts at mild revolt, and I sensed, painfully, for the first time, an idea was quivering in the single soul that the two of us now had, which did not come from me: an idea that came from her.

Finally, one day when we were walking in a fabulous forest, the trees of which were red and the soil blue, a fabulous forest populated with unicorns, hippogriffs, hydras, dragons, sphinxes, chimeras, centaurs, phoenixes and a roc, she let words escape that bruised my soul:

"Lions! Great lions with thunderous roars! To hunt lions . . . !"

---

1 The famous *bains de la Samaritaine*, near the Pont Neuf, disappeared not long after the present story was written, but the name was taken over by an equally-famous department store. Photographs preserved on-line show that the floating baths did indeed have what looks like a black palm tree mounted on the roof; one photograph shows two of them.

"What?" I said to her. "Are we not walking among monsters a thousand times more terrible? Do you not think that the hydra, the dragons and the unicorn are beasts more terrible than all the lions in the world?"

"Yes," she said, "but lions exist . . ."

Oh, when Edwige pronounced those blasphemous words I felt that a part of her soul had fled far from mine, and I began to weep.

And the days went by, clouded with sadness. I felt something like a bleeding wound in the soul, doubtless the wound of some amputated limb, and my soul was so weary and so sad that it no longer had the strength to deploy its wings and fly beyond the native mud.

"Edwige," I said, "why are you becoming estranged from me?"

"You're mistaken," she said.

"No, Edwige, you're thinking about lions, great roaring lions. You're thinking, with your soul of old, that they exist, that they truly exist, and that heroes hunt them."

"That's true," she said, "but it's involuntary. Why have you let me escape? Now, I'd like to know whether heroes exist other than in fables."

"And you'd like to know whether the doctor is one of those living heroes?"

She blushed slightly.

What, in spite of all their seductions and cajoleries, all the ladies of the Bildebières' salon had been unable to do—persuade Doctor Cocon to talk, to explain his mysterious adventure with the lion—I succeeded in doing myself, by means of the simplest of ruses.

One evening, when the doctor was developing a few points if his famous thesis, *Poetry Considered as an Inflammatory and Heredtiary Affection of Certain Tissues in the Fissure of Rolando, its Diagnosis, its Etiology and its Treatment*, I interrupted him.

"If poetry is a malady, Doctor, don't you think that all human beings are born with the germ of that malady—a germ, I admit, rapidly stifled by the majority of people, but nevertheless leaving recognizable traces even in the most prosaic natures? Who, then, I ask you, has not felt at least once the imperious desire for devotion, heroism and flight toward purer and more beautiful elsewheres? Now, are those not the grave symptoms of which you speak yourself, in establishing the diagnosis of the malady in question? Yes, Doctor, every man is born with a poet in him, whom he is generally in haste to strangle. And I would wager that you, Doctor, in a certain epoch, have felt the affliction of the malady you study, that you have been the invalid of which you speak, that you have been a poet."

"Never!" barked the doctor, in the tone of a man cut to the quick by an insult.

"However, Doctor," I said, perfidiously, "do not all these mysterious stories that are whispered about your youth, that scar you bear on your hand, the indelible testimony of old heroisms, these adventures with lions, these thousand actions of sublime folly that one divines in your life, affirm in your past the existence of a state of soul very different from the prosaicism on which you pride yourself today?"

"Never in my life!" barked the indignant doctor, for the second time, white with fury.

"Oh," I said, "don't defend yourself. I love to imagine you in that distant epoch of your existence, disgusted with the flat down-to-earth nature of your everyday life, avid for a more beautiful unknown, avid for heroism, glory and the ideal, for poetry, fleeing toward the distant lands whose strangeness seduced you by virtue of its rapport with the fantastic nature of your dreams, and there, a poet—hear me clearly—a poet in action, hurling yourself recklessly into adventures as terrible as those of a hero of fable, dreaming, like Hercules, of killing hydras and Cyclopes, and resigning yourself, for want of anything better, to struggling at close quarters with lions."

Doctor Cocon bit his lips feverishly. Suddenly, he burst out: "That's insane, Monsieur; your conjectures are insane! Nothing justifies them! Nothing! Nothing! In any case, in order to respond to your wounding accusations, I want to reestablish the facts and recount the episode in my life to which you are alluding, and I take these ladies as my witnesses that the action in question, heroic as it might appear, cannot be accommodated in any fashion to the customary extravagances of the sick individual afflicted with poetic delirium."

All his ladies drew nearer, craning their necks, opening their mouths and ears, at the peak of attention, and I perceived Edwige trembling slightly.

Doctor Cocon commenced his story thus:

"In that epoch, I had just completed my medical studies and had been accepted by the illustrious zoologist Morissot as a laboratory assistant at the Museum of Natural History, in order to aid him, with my feeble observations, to complete his *Monograph on the large African Carnivores Considered as Pests*. In consequence, I hardly quit the menagerie and, in order always to be in proximity with my animals I installed myself in a small room inside the Museum. If some wild animal exhibited any abnormal behavior worthy of being noted, the warden came to wake me up and I ran to see.

"Now, it was spring, and a superb lioness from the Atlas Mountains had just entered into her period of rut. You know, Mesdames, that a lioness in rut has the custom of appealing to the male by means of formidable roars, for which terms of comparison are lacking, and of which all voyagers who have traveled by night in the African deserts speak with terror.

"One night, therefore, the warden came to wake me. The roars of the crazed beast reached me, in spite of the distance, like uninterrupted thunder. 'It's Fatima'—the lioness was named Fatima—"calling for her mate,' the man told me.

"'Very well,' I replied. 'I'll go,'

"It's necessary to tell you, Mesdames, that when a lioness was in a state of rut, it was me, and me alone, who was charged . . ."

"What!" interrupted all the stupefied ladies."It was you? It was you? You alone who were charged . . . ?"

"Exactly. Oh, it wasn't without some trouble and some danger, but you'll see how I went about it . . .

"So, I leapt out of bed, got dressed in haste and ran to the menagerie. Fatima was in a state of indescribable excitement. Her neck extended toward us, her formidable mouth open, she uttered roars vibrant enough to break the windows, and then rolled furiously on the floor of her cage, mewling, howling, and raising her formidable claws toward an invisible assailant.

"I couldn't help saying, in spite of my habitude of the matter: 'Uh oh! This will be difficult.' However, it was necessary to arm myself with courage and decide, for without a doubt, no one in the quarter would get a wink of sleep all night. It's necessary to tell you, Mesdames, for you doubtless don't know these details, that in the floor of the cages of ferocious animals there is a little trapdoor that can be opened to permit the introduction into the cage of solid cables attached to a capstan. Those cables serve to bring down a double metal girdle in the cage. It's a matter—and it's often a long operation—of sliding that double girdle under the belly of the wild beast, which, by means of a very simple mechanism, immediately closes. The warden and I had just encircled the excessively amorous Fatima using that procedure. We then hitched ourselves to the capstan and the beast, roaring harder and harder, was soon suspended fifty centimeters from the floor.

"That wasn't all. It was a mater, with the aid of special chains analogous to those known as cabriolets, of attaching the four feet together, in order to prevent the animal from struggling. That was soon done. Nothing remained but the tail, the redoubtable tail of the beast, which was lashing the air with its terrible whip. We finally succeeded in seizing it and gripping it with a kind of lasso adapted to that purpose, and mooring it to the bars of the cage.

"The preparations were terminated. The animal, suspended from the ceiling, sensing all her limbs paralyzed, understanding the futility of any resistance, waited passively, only roaring feebly. I, Mesdames, had just entered the cage, slightly emotional, I must confess; I approached the hindquarters of the lioness and abruptly, taking advantage of a momentary immobility that had appeared to me to be formidable, I injected her with the bromide solution that I had prepared . . .

"But at that moment . . . what happened, I don't know; all I know is that I suddenly felt the flesh of my hand torn away as if by formidable pincers. Fatima had succeeded in freeing one of her redoubtable paws . . ."

While the doctor was speaking, Edwige had drawn closer to me.

"Forgive me!" she said. "Oh, forgive me! Forgive me . . . !"

And I saw tears moistening her large mauve eyes.

✳

So, I've found you again, Edwige. You've become, once again, my Edwige, since you have been Edwige no longer, but me, and I can talk to you once again, as before, and our amorous conversations will not be a dialogue, a frightful dialogue, but a long and sweet soliloquy . . . for I sense that your soul has really returned to my soul and that your dear speech, for passing through your lips, is nevertheless mine.

"Certainly," she said, "I'm cured forever of going to visit the worlds in which people kill nightingales and medicate lionesses. I want to be nestled forever in the profoundest depths of your beautiful magical soul."

"Do you recall, Edwige, the beautiful river of dream on which we once sailed, in a silver boat with white satin sails, between banks full of palm trees, laburnums, oleanders and miraculous efflorescences?"

"Yes; we were sitting in the prow of the boat, and we let our naked feet dangle, which the foam of the eddies tickled, and we sometimes felt ourselves sinking in sweetness so sharply sweet that we thought we were dying."

"Well. Edwige, would you like to resume that excursion? Here, moored to the bank, is the beautiful silver boat with the white satin sails . . ."

Oh, the foam of the eddies brushing our bare feet . . .

Oh, why, then, did you have, why, then, did we have, the impious desire to come into these accursed realms? Are they the specters of old inhabitants of the drowned cities of the dead sea, these dolorous and lubricious beings, these naked and drunken beings, with foam on their lips, prostituting themselves, in accordance with monstrous fashions, at the crossroads and in the streets of that horrible city with walls of bronze?

Don't you want to flee far away from these abominable spectacles? Already, the bloody gazes of these frenzied individuals have burned our ingenuous flesh with their desires, and already avid hands have reached out toward us. Would it not have been wiser to confine ourselves in the virginal gardens of dream, and not to desire to tread the burning soil of these infernos?

Is it true, then, what a poet once said to me, that the ideal is a dangerous country, with a double aspect, one of azure and the other of night, and that by dint of walking in the magnificence of the azure, there comes a day when one wants to know the sublime horrors of pure darkness, when one feels imperiously attracted by the frightful beauty of absolute ugliness, of the ideal evil?

Oh, Edwige, have we not yielded to that temptation? Let us flee, if there is still time, this city with walls of bronze, where the sniggers of Satan mingle with the voluptuous mewling of satyrs.

"Can we?" said Edwige, sadly. "Is our imprudence not irremediable already? Do you not feel already, as I do, penetrated by the horrible spirit that soars over this somber sky?"

"Alas, yes. Let's try, though."

We have emerged from the terrible city with the walls of bronze, and before us extends a sinister valley dominated by a basalt mountain surmounted by a prodigious temple. It is immense; its walls are painted vermilion; its domes are hammered gold, and a thousand colossal sculpted bronze lions guard its doors.

"Why don't we go into that temple?" said Edwige.

"Oh! I sense, strongly, that it's necessary not to go there."

"However, don't you feel, as I do, an imperious desire to enter it?"

"I have the same imperious desire, alas. But I know that it's necessary not to do it; I sense that it will be terrible."

Edwige fell silent momentarily; then, with her large mauve eyes fixed with desire upon the red walls of the temple, she said: "How are we going to avoid going there? Don't you feel that it will be necessary for us to go there?"

"That's a frightful thought."

"You see," she said, "if it were proposed to you to go away, to flee far from that temple, you'd respond that our feet are nailed to the ground, that your gaze is riveted to those red walls."

"That's true; I truly can no longer draw away, and I can see that we're doomed, forever doomed."

"I also have that presentiment, but perhaps we're mistaken. In sum, it's only a presentiment, and since it's also impossible, absolutely impossible, not to go there, let's risk the adventure; let's go, friend, let's march . . ."

Eyes still fixed upon the scarlet walls, we have commenced climbing the basalt mountain . . .

"Edwige, you will have wanted it."

"And you, Hans, will you not have wanted it? Could we have not wanted it?"

"Edwige, can you feel how I'm trembling?"

We crossed the threshold of the formidable iron door guarded by colossal lions sculpted in bronze. Under the enormous vaults painted in gold and red lead, at the foot of a thousand statues of monstrous gods with the ferocious jaws of carnivorous beasts, a furious crowd is rolling and howling over the porphyry paving-stones furrowed by scarlet streams. On every side, mounted on crimsoned altars, priests naked to the waist, their foreheads coiffed with tiaras of fabulous gems, are cutting the throats of human victims with golden cutlasses, and, at intervals, raising their red arms and their red hands toward the sky, full of bleeding entrails, from which warm blood is streaming over the naked flesh of their shoulders and their breasts.

I turned toward Edwige and looked at her for a long time, with eyes that I sensed were hostile.

"You will have wanted it! You will have wanted it!" I repeated, in a voice that seemed to me to be as hoarse as a bark.

The horrible furious crowd, the horrible crowd ablaze with an unspeakable delight, had precipitated toward the altars. From all sides the priests threw them the immolated cadavers, and all of them hurled themselves upon a human rag like famished dogs hurling themselves upon their portion of a kill. Infernal howls made the walls and the golden cupolas tremble. There were horrible battles over who would tear a morsel of flesh from the victim, battles in which fingernails and teeth broke in flesh, and the glint of blades sometimes shone in the darkness; and in that crowd of new victims there were some who were gasping, their throats slashed, and upon whom, again and always, others threw themselves, disemboweling them, butchering them and devouring them.

"Are you mad, Edwige? Are you mad?"

Is it a vision? Is it a nightmare? Ah! Now she too, my blonde, my white Edwige, has thrown herself, like a famished bitch, grinding her teeth, into that human butchery, and she too is disputing her share of the meat, and she is rolling and howling in that blood, in all that blood . . .

"Your white stockings, Edwinge? Why do you no longer have your white stockings? Why are your stockings red? Why are they so red?"

Oh, what delirium is making her writhe, making her howl, like that? Will I be able to see her fingernails and teeth tearing those shreds for much longer? And me, and me, am I drunk? Am I not also on my knees amid that blood, do I not have hands full of blood, and am I not disputing with Edwige a morsel of flesh? Oh, now I've thrown myself upon her, mad, eyes bloody, on her on my beloved, and now I'm knocking her down, and tearing with my teeth at her throat, her white throat . . .

"Oh, yes, yes!" she gasps, "kill me, I want you to kill me, I want you to see my blood flow, I want to be the naiad of a river of blood . . ."

And, howling, I have dragged her by the hair to the nearest altar, and I have snatched the golden cutlass from the hands of the priest, and I have stabbed Edwige in the naked breast, and the blood has spurted like a spray of rubies all the way to my face, and the blood has blinded me.

"Again! Again!" gasps Edwige. "I want to see my blood. I want it to flow upon the ground in a great red river . . .

"Again!"

It's really finished. Edwige is dead. Edwige is dead!

Doctor Cocon has come to certify the decease. The engineer Bildebières accompanied him. They have both shaken my hand, with grimaces of compunction and banal phrases of condolence.

"My poor friend . . . It's a great misfortune . . . To die so young . . . But in the end, there must be a reason . . ."

Afterwards, Doctor Cocon explained the causes of Edwige's death at length. According to him, she died of meningitis, and I am, in large measure, responsible for the malady that carried her away. My friend's little brain, it appears, was too weak for the debauches of the imagination that I imposed on it. The overwork of the cerebral cells determined the congestion of certain tissues, a terrible inflammation of the meninges, and when the illness takes on that character, science is impotent . . .

"Oh, young man, say now, then, that poetry is not a malady, a malady from which one can die!"

I have killed Edwige. Oh, I know only too well that I have killed Edwige. But I also know full well that she did not die of a banal meningitis, since I plunged the great cutlass of the priest of Moloch into her breast twenty times over.

✳

"Go and rest for a while," the engineer Bildebières said to me. "We'll watch over her, Doctor Cocon and I. About midnight, when you've slept for a while, you can come to replace us. The doctor will go home, but I'll stay here to sleep, for I don't want to leave you alone in such a dolorous circumstance."

He doesn't want to leave me alone, and I know why. Yesterday, in a crisis of despair, I tried to kill myself on Edwige's cadaver, and in spite of all weapons having been confiscated, in spite of my having sworn not to do it again, the engineer isn't tranquil; he intends to watch over me.

I yielded to his entreaties, and while they installed themselves in armchairs I went into the next room to lie down on a divan.

Alas, I had no desire to sleep, and as the door had remained open I was annoyed to hear the impious conversation of my two friends. They had started to talk about Edwige, initially eulogistically, with some commiseration.

"It's very young to die . . ."

"She was so good and gentle . . ."

"And truly intelligent. Do you remember the witty thing she said to us one evening when we were discussing woman?"

But gradually, restrictions crept into the praise, like snakes.

"It's necessary to admit, though, that she was a bit mad."

"Yes, she had a weak head, and Hans finished off troubling it with his divagations."

"Do you think that she was truly very intelligent?"

"I don't think so."

"He could have found a more intelligent, more serious woman."

"And more beautiful."

"Oh, yes, for she certainly wasn't beautiful."

"No, at the most she had a certain strange *je ne sais quoi* in her physiognomy that could be seductive."

"Oh, and how. Personally, I found her rather ugly."

"Yes, she was rather ugly."

"And then, with that, she wasn't very young."

"No, what age would you give her?"

"I don't know, but personally, I like women younger than that."

"That's like me! I remember, when I came out of the École, I had a gamine of sixteen for a mistress . . . people called her Chochotte. Oh, if you had seen the two of us at the balls of the day, dancing the cancan, as people knew how to dance it in those days! She took off my hat with a kick with such facility! One evening, I remember . . ."

And they started recounting in detail funny and lewd stories that they recalled from their youth. And while I was weeping in the room next door, while I was biting the pillows of the divan to stifle my sobs. I heard their bawdy anecdotes, continually punctuated by bursts of ill-contained laughter.

At midnight I came, as agreed, to relieve them of that impious guard. Doctor Cocon retired, the engineer Bildebières went to lie down in the next room, on the divan that I had just quit.

Oh, how beautiful she was thus, my dear Edwige, rigidly stretched out on that bed, evocative of magical sensual pleasures, so pale, with a mysterious smile on her white lips, truly marmoreal in pallor and rigidity.

I had dressed her in the foulard dress with extinct colors that she had been wearing the first evening I saw her. I had piously covered her legs in the pretty white stockings that she loved, and her small slender feet in light green pumps, and on the bed on which she lay I had strewn lilies, forget-me-nots and tea-roses . . .

I wept for a long, long time, kneeling beside her. I kissed the mysterious smile on her cold lips desperately, and her cold forehead, and her cold hands, and her little cold feet. And I felt a kind of choking sensation within me, at not being able, in a language rich enough, to pour out the dolor with which my soul was full, when I perceived my harpsichord in a corner, my old harpsichord of yesteryear, with the crystal and golden voice. Oh, how I threw myself upon its yellow ivory, where my tears rained down, and how I sang the heart-rending hymn if my despair . . .

Oh, Edwige, the heart-rending sobs, the sublime lamentations of the song of mourning that my inspired fingers were able to extract from the marvelous harpsichord, your eyes, your beautiful mauve eyes—I believed so, at least—will they not open one last time?

"Come on, shut up!" said the engineer, surging into the room. "Word of honor, it's indecent!"

✳

Why weep? Why should I weep for Edwige? Why should I weep for having killed her?

In killing her, in the red sky, have I not liberated her?

Now, she has reentered the heaven of pure ideas. I might encounter her there, in the corner of some dream, and then, it will be her, undoubtedly, her, an imponderable dragonfly with wings of dream, who will take pity on me, who will take pity on the heavy snail who is attempting to scale the azure.

And then, why should I regret the thousand times deceptive appearance that she was? Do I not know the secret of recreating her, the secret of metamorphosing her into the Edwige that she was, the first woman who could pass by without refusing to put her hand in mine.

And yet . . . ! And yet . . . ! Whence comes this sadness that remains within me pitilessly? Do I not have some sin to expiate? Have I not been too egotistical? Am I not too complicit in these solitary exaltations, and is it not a crime to have been so scornful of the poor fraternal creatures who are obstinate in crawling in the natal mud?

Do I not owe to them a part of my joys?

Oh, henceforth I want to expiate that sin of egotism by an immense pity. I want my poor brothers of the muddy streams to participate, thanks to me, in the celestial joys that I know. I want to bring them back from heaven the luminous and perfumed rays stolen from the corollas of stats, and I want all of them to bless me as a sublime benefactor.

Edwige! Edwige! you who are floating now in the pure essence of beauty, inspire me with the genius necessary to translate the marvelous verities into the language of appearances, breathe into me the words that are necessary, direct my brushes, tune my lyre! I want to reveal to them, to my poor brothers of the muddy stream, the happiness of the azures that we have explored. Edwige, make of me a Homer, a Leonardo da Vinci, a Wagner, that men might bless me forever for all the joys that I will have revealed to their eyes and their ears!

Two formidable bursts of laughter interrupted me. It was Doctor Cocon and the engineer Bildebières, who were listening to me without my noticing.

"My poor boy," said the engineer, "if you have no benefits to lavish on humankind more solid than that, don't count too much on their gratitude."

AVELINE

THERE was once a young woman named Aveline. She was so beautiful and so gentle, with her large eyes the color of forget-me-nots, her flesh as pale as milk and her long hair, almost white, that the local youths, although they were not poets, took her for an angel who had lost the way to Paradise.

One day, when Aveline, in a white dress, with her almost-white hair floating over her shoulders, was in the garden picking lilies, Our Lord Jesus Christ, who chanced to be walking in the realm, happened to pass by on the road. Over the hawthorn hedge in flower, he perceived the beautiful and gentle young woman, very white, among the lilies of the garden.

He stopped to contemplate her, and as a local youth was passing along the road at that moment, he asked him who the young woman was, so beautiful and so gentle, with large eyes the color of forget-me-nots, flesh the color of milk and long hair, almost white.

"Lord," the local youth replied, "her name is Aveline, but she's undoubtedly not a young woman, but an angel who has lost the way to Paradise."

Our Lord Jesus Christ went away, very pensive, and did not take long to rise into Heaven again. He went to find his father, who was sitting on his golden throne and caressing his long white beard, while listening to the sublime songs that the choirs of cherubim were singing.

"Father," he said, "I've seen a young woman on earth whose name is Aveline. She's so beautiful and so gentle, with large eyes the color of forget-me-nots, her flesh as pale as milk and her long hair, almost white, that the local youths, although they aren't poets, all take her for an angel who has lost the way to Paradise. Father, she was all white among the lilies of the garden, and I too believe that she isn't a young woman, but an angel who has lost the way to Paradise. Why, Father, since she is worthy of it, do we not open Heaven to her and give her for companions the angels who are her brothers?"

"If it would please you, my son—but I fear that it might have unfortunate results, for, in the final analysis, women are not angels."

"Oh, Father, if you had seen her, all white, among the lilies of her garden . . . !"

"All right, my son, try."

Lord Jesus Christ descended from Heaven again into the land where Aveline lived.

She was in her thatched cottage, making up a bouquet of the lilies she had picked, and she had put a few of them in her almost-white hair.

"Aveline," he said to her, "you are not a young woman, you are an angel who has lost the way to Paradise."

"Lord," she said, simply, "everyone repeats that to me, but truly, I don't know anything about it."

"Follow me, Aveline. I will open the door to Heaven for you, where you were doubtless born, and I shall return you to the company of the angels, your brothers."

They departed together, and Our Lord Jesus Christ went back up to Heaven, carrying her in his arms.

She did not feel at all out of place. All day long she amused herself walking in the azure, lying down on the beautiful clouds, listening to the divine music of the cherubim and talking to the angels. They all watched her running in the celestial enclosures, so beautiful and so gentle, with her eyes the color of forget-me-nots, her flesh as pale as milk and her long almost-white hair starred with lilies, and they all wondered what that angel was that they had never seen before in Paradise.

She sang the praises of the Almighty with them, with her voice, so soft and so pure; she drank nectar with them from golden cups, which, as everyone knows, is the delicious wine produced by the vines that grow in Heaven.

"Was I not right, Father?" said Our Lord. "Was Aveline not made to live among our celestial phalanges?"

"Let's wait and see, my son. I'm afraid that nothing good will come of all this."

And, sitting in his golden throne, the Almighty started caressing his long white beard, only listening with a distracted ear to the sublime songs that the choirs of cherubim were singing.

✳

Meanwhile, it had already been a day, an entire day, since Aveline had penetrated into Heaven and had been savoring the ineffable sensual pleasures of Paradise. Was she weary of celestial felicities? She was no longer playing with the angels, she was no longer singing the praises of the Almighty with them, in her voice that was so soft and so pure. She seemed anxious. A slight frown disturbed the tranquility of her pale face, and she sometimes bit her lip nervously. She walked in the azure nervously, making a tour of every cloud, and seemed irritated by finding angels, archangels and cherubim everywhere, playing or singing.

In the end, as if in a fit of despair, she stopped one of them by seizing his azure robe and, leaning toward his ear, she started whispering to him. He seemed very astonished, and replied: "I don't know . . . I don't understand . . ."

And when she persisted, he could only repeat: "I don't understand . . . I don't know what you mean . . . I've never heard mention of that."

Then Aveline drew away and began to weep. Everyone looked at her, for they had never seen weeping in Paradise.

Our Lord Jesus Christ, who was sitting to the right of his father, perceived her in tears, and made her a sign to approach him.

"What!" he said to her. "You're weeping, Aveline? You're weeping in Paradise? What's the matter with you, Aveline?"

"Lord," she said, "it's doubtless the nectar, all the nectar I've drunk . . . and the angels don't want to tell me . . ."

She interrupted herself to burst into sobs, and as Our Lord Jesus Christ did not understand either, she was obliged to lean toward his ear and whisper to him, blushing, what she had said to the angels.

"Aveline, Aveline," said Our Lord, sadly, "can you not live with us in Paradise, then? The angels are unaware of these vile needs; are you not, as I believed, similar to the angels?"

"Lord, Lord," said Aveline sobbing, "if I can't relieve myself in Paradise, it's necessary that I leave. It's necessary that I leave. Please transport me back to earth, to my little garden where the lilies grow . . . for truly, I can't wait any longer, I can't wait any longer."

Aveline has returned to earth. She is walking again, all white, among the lilies of the garden, and the local youths, although they are not poets, when they perceive her, so beautiful and so gentle, her large eyes the color of forget-me-nots, her flesh as pale as ilk and her long hair, almost white, above the flowering hawthorn hedge, never fail to take her for an angel who has lost the way to Paradise.

And all the poets too, who have come from distant cities, to which the reputation of her celestial beauty has flown, when they perceive her, so beautiful and so gentle, with her large eyes the color of forget-me-nots, her flesh as pale as milk and her long, almost-white hair, above the hedge of flowering hawthorn, occupied in picking lilies in her garden, never fail to say to her, in their pretty songs, that she is an angel who has lost the way to Paradise.

But she is content to look at them with a mysterious smile, for she knows full well now that she is not an angel, not an angel at all.

THE ANCESTRESS

WHEN Léon Lécuyer penetrated into the amorous little drawing room where little Charlotte d'Albreuse was accustomed to hold the informal sessions of her quotidian five o'clocks—in the amorous little drawing room draped with delicate shiny satin and plush in pastel shades, and furnished with the pretty and exquisite ugliness that constitutes what the archeologists of the future will denominate as the purest "rococotte style"—the dainty mistress of the house, half-lying face down among the multicolored cushions of a divan more Oriental than necessary, raised her pert, thin, smiling pink face cheerfully.

"Oh, dear Léon, how nice of you to come and see me . . . it's been such a long time!"

Then, turning toward a person of incalculable age, sprawled like a vague pile of rags in the depths of a settee: "Come on, Baba! Offer an armchair to Monsieur Lécuyer!"

As soon as he was seated, she said: "Tell me . . . you'll have a cup of tea, won't you?"

"Yes, of course . . . with pleasure, my dear . . . you'll permit me to call you by your pet name . . . my dear Rigolette . . ."

"Oh, that joke! If I permit! Baba, bring a cup of tea . . . and rum? You'll have rum in it, eh? Baba! Put some rum in it . . . you can smoke, you know . . . Baba! Go fetch the cigarettes . . . or would you prefer a cigar? Baba! The cigars . . . Baba! Matches . . . Baba! The small ash-tray . . ."

The person addressed obeyed, carrying out all her orders with hasty, stupid awkwardness. He was a fellow about forty years of age, as dilapidated as an octogenarian. He walked, dancing grotesquely, with an ataxic gait, his hands swinging, his spine curved and his head minuscule, hairless, jaundiced, wrinkled, faded and shriveled, like the head of a guinea-fowl, dangling and shaking at the end of an immeasurable neck, frail and flaccid.

Before he had been nicknamed Baba, for equivocal reasons now forgotten, his name had been Vicomte Georges d'Albefort.

"Baba! Pass the little cakes, then . . . ! Baba! A sugar-lump . . ."

Once, in the days of his relative splendor, he had been Charlotte's official lover, and so much her official lover that he had let her ruin him like an imbecile. As soon as his discomfiture had led to him being thrown out, as is normal and just, the poor unfortunate, already more than half-dotard, his spinal marrow diseased and his meager brain irremediably softened by absurd youthful sprees, and, in spite of all that, more amorously besotted than ever, had been desperate, had moaned, sobbed, wept, prayed, begged, so much that little La d'Albreuse, finally taking pity, consented to open her door to him again, no longer, certainly, in the quality of lover but that of old comrade, in the hour when she received . . . everyone!"

"Baba! A biscuit . . . ! Give me my little spoon! Baba! Close the door, then. . ."

She had made of the pitiful cretin a kind of semi-flunkey, executing for her all the thousand minuscule tasks of the idle life; and he, humble, fearful, shrunken, like a lame lap-dog tolerated in a drawing room, remained huddled in his little corner, happy to have the right to contemplate her and scent her, happy to save her the enormous fatigue of extending her arm toward a cup, hastening, at every word, with comically zealous awkwardness, submitting, head bowed, without flinching, in order not to be thrown out, to the harshest and bloodiest humiliations and the most insulting rebuffs.

"Baba! Light the candelabra . . . ! One can no longer see clearly . . . good! Imbecile! He's broken another candlestick . . . oh, by the way, Lécuyer . . . let me tell you a story . . . a story! Oh, but a story to make one die laughing!"

"Go on, I'm listening."

"You know my fat baron?"

"Which one? Machin? Steesinger? The banker? You're still with him?"

"Well, of course! Baba, you're insupportable, sniffing like that! Well, can you imagine that my silly baron . . ."

She interrupted herself, uttered a loud burst of bright laughter, one of those bursts of open-mouthed laughter that only women proud of an indisputable dentition practice.

"No! You see . . . Léon . . . ! No! It's too funny . . . it's too silly . . .I could never . . . tell you . . ."

Madly, she buried her pink nose in the cushions, continuing to writhe on the divan.

Lécuyer and Baba looked at one another, laughing at seeing her laugh, and both of them were charmed and slightly stimulated by the joyful and fantastic convulsions of the pretty and dainty female body in its mischievous gamine elegance, shaken by that indescribable hilarity, quivering and palpitating.

"Oh," said Lécuyer, "you're an artful one, my dear! You know that you're never more charming than when you show your pretty teeth!"

And, in fact, she was impossibly exquisite thus, her snowy little teeth sparkling between her slightly thick scarlet lips, her cheeks carmined, her blue eyes moist, washed by teas of laughter, her breasts jiggled by spasms—very exquisite, and well worthy of the fresh, foolish and youthful pet name of Rigolette with which the people of her society had dubbed her. And certainly, anyone who had credited her with her true age would have been very malign, for—it can be said, since she laughed at it herself sometimes—little La d'Albreuse, the pert gamine, so mischievous, so youthful, was no longer very young!

But the inept gossip columnist of some great daily newspaper who had taken it into his head one day, out of rancorous jealousy, to qualify her as "old guard" had only made her shrug her shoulders. Old guard! She laughed for a week. Yes, doubtless, she counted thirty-nine years. Thirty-nine years well chimed, at least three years ago, but was she not still ideally pretty? Did she not still possess that enticing childish pertness, that aperitif freshness of green fruits? In spite of the spree commenced in her fifteenth year, in spite of her double maternity, was she not still and forever the same pink and cheerful girl, without a wrinkle at her temples, without a white hair in her blonde fleece, without a millimeter more round her waist? Had she not all the pearls of her gums, her cheeks as rosy as a virgin's, her small breasts as hard as agate?

"That's true," Baba confirmed. "Yes, that's true. She's charming when she laughs."

"Come on, no insolence," said Charlotte, finally almost calm. "No insolence, Baba! And pass me the cigarettes. Can you imagine then . . . that my cretin of a baron . . . oh, no, it's too funny . . . I . . . oh, let me laugh! Can you imagine . . . that he took it into his head, the other day . . . to be jealous . . . to be jealous . . ."

"Of whom?"

"Of whom? Of Baba! Yes, my dear, of Baba . . . ! Of Baba . . . ! Ha ha ha ha!"

Again, she laughed, writhing in a formidable and clownish crisis of mad laughter, half-choking, her abdomen convulsed, her eyelashes streaming, beating the air with her arms and legs.

"Can you imagine . . . I'd had supper . . . with little Henri. Do you know Henri . . . my little Henri? I came home late . . . very late . . . the following day, at noon. Then, when Baba came, I was still in bed. I said to him: 'Baba, I'm going to get up . . . you can double as my chambermaid . . . Baba! put on my stockings . . . ! Baba! my garters . . . ! Baba! take off my nightdress . . . Baba!

go fetch me a day chemise . . . there, in the cupboard . . . on the second shelf . . . the mauve surah!' And bang! It was at that moment that the baron came in! Tableau! I was sitting on the bed . . . stark naked, it's true . . . but in front of Baba, you understand! It was insignificant . . . Baba isn't a man! Well, that imbecile of a baron . . . that imbecile of a baron . . ."

"A telegram for Madame!" interjected Jack, Charlotte's groom-factotum, at that moment.

And the insolent gamin with the head of a bulldog, pretentiously clad in fine azure cloth and silk stockings, handed the dispatch to his mistress.

She scanned the blue paper with her eyes. Her shoulders twitched, and she suddenly went very pale, biting her lip.

"Bad news?" asked Lécuyer.

Charlotte did not reply.

With nervous fingers she crumpled the telegram and, frowning, fixing a distant vision with a hateful, harsh gaze, she leaned forward, grimly mute, her chin in her little hand, which was trembling.

Annihilated, as if overwhelmed by the shock of a suddenly-revealed formidable malaise, she remained thus, her brain dead and her tongue frozen, forgetting her visitor, unconscious of everything.

That silence, in the end, became embarrassing. Léon repeated: "You've received some bad news . . . ?"

She still did not appear to have heard anything, but her fixed eyes suddenly became brighter, bright with a vague reflection of dampness; her eyelids fluttered, like the wings of a little dying bird, and two large tears, as luminous as diamonds, filtered between her long lashes, the color of saffron, and then rolled over the pallor of her cheeks.

Léon Lecuyer stood up, afraid of being indiscreet, bowed and went away, muttering into his moustache: "Zut! Rigolette weeping now! That's never been seen! What can possibly have happened?"

Also full of stupor, and of alarm and solicitude, Baba had approached the divan, frightened, losing his head—the little that he had, at least—moaning humble questions and desolate and infantile consolations . . .

Suddenly, and for all response, La d'Albreuse buried her head in her hands and burst into tears. After those minutes of tragic mutism, it was like a terrible explosion. Writhing in terrible convulsions of hysteria, bruising her flesh on the walls, lacerating the plush of the cushions with her frail clenched fingers, grinding her teeth, she filled the drawing room with moans, lamentations, cries of rage and howls.

Terrified, Baba knelt down beside her, weeping like her, dabbing her eyes with a handkerchief, caressing her awkwardly, begging her, interrogating her, in a coaxing, heart-broken, stammering, tremulous, comically anguished voice.

"Charlotte . . . my little Charlotte . . . oh, don't cry . . . ! don't cry!"

And abruptly, emboldened, intoxicated by emotion, lit up by an audacity of desperation, he seized her temples in his poor heavy hands, and, in order to console her, piously, maternally, he kissed her eyelids.

At the contact of Baba's flaccid lips and viscous flesh, La d'Albreuse straightened up with an abrupt bound, indignant and repugnant. She gave him a slap, which sank into the soft adiposity of the poor dotard as if into gelatine, and cried, her teeth clenched and her speech hissing and strident: "Swine! Dirty swine! Get out! Get out . . . !"

Then, changing her mind, that anger having had the action of an effective remedy on her dolor, she said: "No! Stay . . . ! Stay, Baba . . . ! My poor Baba! Stay! I'll tell you everything . . . I'll tell you why I'm weeping . . . because, in sum . . . you're stupid, but you're not nasty, you, Baba! Only, you see, Baba, it's necessary that you swear to me . . . not to repeat anything. You understand, Baba? And then, also . . . it's necessary to promise me . . . to answer truthfully . . . truthfully . . . to what I ask of you. You understand, Baba? You have to promise me . . ."

Moved to tears by the uncustomary and sympathetic confidence, the dotard stammered solemn oaths.

"Baba! Lock the door," said Charlotte.

Then she held out her foot to him.

"Baba! Take off my slippers . . ."

He knelt down, religiously, while she wiped away furtive tears that were still pearling at the end of her eyelashes.

"Baba! Take off my stockings . . ."

When her legs were bare, she leapt on to the divan, standing upright.

With slow gestures, she set about unfastening her peignoir, and threw it in a corner. Then it was the turn of the corset. She took out the pins retaining her chignon, and her heavy yellow hair collapsed and rolled over her hips.

In Baba's atonal and bleary eyes, an unusual gleam shone. He gazed with all his might, fascinated, charmed, ecstatic, stupefied, indelibly rapturous.

Suddenly, with a brisk flick, she let her chemise slide down to her ankles.

There was then an abrupt and, so to speak, phantasmagorical surge of the most impossibly pretty of nudities, the sudden apparition of an admirable flamboyance of flesh, as hard and smooth as nacre, as white as ink and shiny as dreamlike satin. And the profile of her exquisitely neat forms, such delicate fragilities of adolescence, outlined against the cerulean plush of the wall like a statue petrified from gems and light, a radiant statue whose two small breasts tipped by two red dots had quivered with recent sobs.

Stupid with admiration, incapable of proffering a word, Baba gaped.

Then, very grave, in a sad tone punctuated by dolorous sobs, Charlotte d'Albreuse said: "Baba! Am I not still beautiful? Tell me the truth, Baba . . . am I still beautiful? You see, Baba, I'm . . . I'm forty-two . . . I'll be forty-three in five months . . . but I'm still beautiful, aren't I? As fresh, as pretty as . . . when you knew me . . . you know, Baba, the first time? I was playing Cupid . . . at the Bouffes . . . oh, it was a long time ago! Isn't it true, Baba, that I'm . . . as young as if I were sixteen?"

The dotard exclaimed, announcing admiring affirmations, and, the seizure awakening in him a cerebral effort of which one would not have thought him capable, he conceived and formulated a comparison with Venus.

Charlotte went on, in a duller, jerky voice intercut mid-phrase by sobs: "Well, now, Baba . . . since I think . . . that you've been frank . . . I . . . I'll tell you . . . I'll tell you why I'm weeping . . . why . . . why I have a desire to kill myself . . . oh, you see . . . Baba . . . my poor Baba . . . I don't know . . . if you'll understand . . . but . . . it's horrible. Oh, it's horrible . . ."

Tears came to her eyes again, urgent, running over her cheeks, dripping on to her breasts, sliding all the way over the nudity of her thighs in little shiny streams. Nervously, she bruised her flesh, her fists thumping the gilded nape of her neck, tearing at her hair.

"Oh, Baba!" she went on, moaning, speaking in hiccups. "Baba! How I'm suffering . . . finally . . . it's necessary, all the same . . . that I tell you. Baba! Listen . . . that telegram . . . that telegram . . . you know? That telegram I received . . . it announces . . . it announces . . . oh no! It's frightful. It's frightful! Oh . . ."

And, howling a cry of desperate rage, she let herself fall, collapsing on to the divan, half-mad, her nerves taut, beating the wall with her head, her feet and her fists, her breast heaving with sobs, choking, gasping, shaken by convulsive hiccups, her teeth chattering, her eyes, like burst clouds, pouring out a deluge of tears.

And then there were Baba's terrors, his emotional and maladroit zeal, his infantile consolations, his vain idiotic solicitudes, his dabbing of the dear eyelids . . .

But suddenly, bracing her will, by virtue of a prodigious effort, stamping on her dolor in order to make it shut up, Rigolette straightened up, wiped away her tears, and, with a frightful calmness, in a harsh, hollow, strident

voice, which, it was evident, everything that a human being can contain of suffering and despair was mastered
and concentrated, her jaws clenched, she proffered,
slowly:

"That telegram . . . that telegram . . . announces to me
that . . . I'm a grandmother!"

Very pale, her eyebrows frowning, her eyes haggard
with madness, in a frightful fixity, riveted to a distant and
odious vision, she remained thus, stark naked, wallowing
and prostrate among the torn and crumpled cushions,
her chin in her clenched hand, rolling in her little skull a
seething broth of sinister ideas . . .

Baba, very troubled, understanding the necessity of
finding a consolatory phrase, a word worthy of the trag-
edy, proportionate to the dolorous situation, interrogated
his poor, obstinately mute brain, effortfully.

Finally, approaching Charlotte respectfully, he tapped
her on the cheek, and stammered, in a very emotional
tone: "There, there, baby . . . baby . . ."

PLUTUS

WHILE the men of today hurl the honey of their hypocrisy toward Heaven, and, wallowing in the royal luxury of their houses, their hands bathed in the gold of coffers, priding themselves on their disinterest and scorn for vile riches;

While they spit ingrate blasphemies in your face, old Plutus, and clamor your infamy in the streets, and affect disdain for the presents with which you heap them;

Alone, my head held high, I will kneel publicly in your golden temple, a ragged vagabond, before your diamond idol.

Proudly, I will make you my humble prayer, unique contenter of human desire. Without deigning to listen to the mockery of the crowd, I will implore your divine blindness and I will kiss your feet, like an old beggar.

I will say to you: "Father of all joys and all virtues, sovereign effacer of crime and remorse, sole God of the world, be propitious to me. Let me draw gold and gems from the sumptuous and inexhaustible cellars of your mercy.

"Let your charity flow in my house like a Pactolus that never runs dry.

"Open to me the doors of hermetic caverns, enable me to possess piles of gold, silver, pearls, rubies, sapphires, amethyst, emeralds, topazes and diamonds as high as the Himalayas, that I might be rich enough to buy the universe!"

And if ever, eccentric idol, you grant my prayer, I will intoxicate you with myrrh and incense, I will sing you marvelous hymns, I will immolate on your altars all innocences, all virtues, all grandeurs and all virginities; I will not be a shameful devotee; I will practice uniquely the cruel rites that please you, I will combat the angels with your golden sword. I will be your prophet, O divine corrupter!

I will live in a palace of dream. My palace will be full of distant music. Artistes will come to offer me the flowers of their hearts. Women will come, naked and perfumed, to present me with the flower of their bodies. Kings will be my valets. I shall buy amour from the queens of the night. And I will be a God, except for immortality.

While the men of today hurl the honey of their hypocrisy toward Heaven, and, wallowing in the royal luxury of their houses, their hands bathed in the gold of coffers, priding themselves on their disinterest and scorn for vile riches;

I will be your prophet, O divine suborner! I will be a poet. I will sing your glory loudly, your power and your goodness, I will say canticles of amour to you.

In order to sate your appetites as a corruptor god, I will make myself the great Sower of Evil. I will sub-

sidize crime and treason. I will be the apostle of Vice,
Depravity and Damnation. I will be a seducer, I will cor-
rupt innocence, virtue and goodness.

I will make so much wealth flow over the earth that
humankind will soon starve to death in the midst of an
immense desert of gold.

Old Plutus, father of all joys and all virtues, sovereign
effacer of crime and remorse, only God of the word, be
propitious to me!

THE BLUE WOMAN

AS I searched for the supreme and unrealizable amour in the obscure maze of the shames of Paris, I arrived, weary and desperate, on one of those lustful sepulchers where bare-breasted courtesans prowl.

And I was about to fall asleep in my desperation, as in a sinister catafalque, when I perceived, leaning on the white satin of a divan, the impossible woman once glimpsed in vague aspirations.

A cruel joy suddenly grew within me, and crazy frissons of desire burned my marrow, for I had before my eyes the beloved stranger, so long an object of hope, the unique, maddening, marvelous, monstrous, sublime, seraphic, divine phenomenon: the blue woman.

She let her satin chemise slide to the ground, and when she was naked, I saw that the flesh of her body had the pure and soft color of the pale azure skies of the morning.

Her large eyes shone like pure sapphires; her cheeks and the tips of her breasts had the joyful and vivid hue of cobalt.

Her hair was as fleecy over her celestial neck as the ultramarine of African seas, and her speech had the ineffable blue tint of forget-me-nots.

And when, on the satin of divans, I had embraced the blue woman for a long time, when I had learned from her monstrous kisses unknown on earth, I planted my trenchant teeth in her azure neck, in order that no one else would ever savor that superhuman sensuality; I saw the fuming indigo of her blood flowing over her flanks as caressant as the pale azure of a morning sky, and I saw her soul, as blue as the flame of sulfur, fly away toward the eternal blueness.

And since then I have wept, in the banal alcoves of white women, for the irredeemable loss of my life.

PRIDE

I love you and I understand you, presumptuous monks who sleep in coffins, who grow old in cilices and bruise your flesh with the lead of discipline.

I love you and I understand you, arrogant martyrs who march to the torture with hearts overflowing with joy. You, Regulus, who allowed your eyelids to be torn away; you, Sebastian, who were overwhelmed by arrows and stones; you, Scevola, who plunged your hand into a brazier; all of you, haughty virgins who were eaten by beasts in Latin circuses; and you, Christ, sublimely contemptuous of executioners!

I love you and I understand you, all of you, divinely proud, joyfully tortured, great seekers of the unknown, for, while your naked limbs were bleeding in tortionary engines, your hearts were swooning in infallible sensualities, and, proud of their impassive pride, knew the happiness of suffering, the suffering of sensing their bodies die.

BELSHAZZAR'S FEAST: A FANTASIA

WELL, YES! Well, yes, by the pure ivory of your impeccable calf, this tale, Madame, and very indubitably, exquisite lectrice, this tale, which was narrated to me once long ago—oh, very long ago—in some nebulous desert, by my friend Chonchinette—you know, Chonchinette, that little indecent Chonchinette who speaks like she loves—this tale, then, is not very moral, and is very scabrous to relate . . . so immoral and so scabrous, truly, that I hesitate to repeat it to you . . .

Aren't you going to blush? blush with virtuous shame? blush all the way to the pretty dimples in your knees? I can already hear you excommunicating me with a terrible: "Oh, fie! The vile writer!"

But bah! Let's see. For once . . . just for this once, be indulgent! Listen to the peppery badinage of Chonchinette without pinching your charming pert madder-red lips, listen, deign to listen with a smile, since no one is looking at you. No?

In the time of La Lavallière and La Pompadour, the great ladies of the court, your ancestresses were hardly accustomed to affect grim prudishness in similar circum-

stances. And yet, no one is surely unaware that the good
La Fontaine did not spare, for them, pimento or red pep-
per in the stew of his amorous anecdotes. Did that, I ask
you, prevent him from being esteemed by Madame de
La Sablière, becoming classic and absolutely usual in all
young ladies' boarding schools?

And what about Monsieur Pavillon? You don't know
Monsieur Pavillon? Monsieur Pavillon of the Académie
Française? Monsieur Pavillon was a worthy man who
had composed a poem—only one poem, but a sublime
poem, an indescribable and hilarious poem entitled *The
Metamorphosis of Iris's Bum into a Star*.[1]

"Oh, fie! The vile word . . ."

Your amiable grandmothers, Madame, your witty
grandmothers, were not annoyed by it, did not blush at
it. Oh, far from it! They laughed instead, they laughed,
the little rascals, until they wet the satins and brocades
of their lovely panel skirts. But that's not all. They ended
up finding the lewd joke so good that they plotted to
seat its witty author in the first vacant armchair under
Mazarin's cupola. And, as you can well imagine, in such
dainty handcuffs, the affair was quickly settled!

Certainly, I have no ambition to be, any day soon,
like La Fontaine, the favorite classic of boarding-school
demoiselles, and I have no hope that these pages, inspired

---

1 Étienne Pavillon (1632-1705), was, indeed, credited posthumous-
ly, but doubtless apocryphally, with writing a story in verse entitled
"*Métamorphose du cul d'Iris changé en astre*." His published works,
which actually served as a (very slender) qualification for admission
to the Académie, include "*Le Portrait du pur amour*" [The Portrait of
Pure Love] (1687), dedicated "*à l'insensible Iris*." which presumably
inspired the satirical attribution.

in me by that little blonde devil Chonchinette, will open the forbidding gates of the Institut to me tomorrow. Today, a poem, no matter how hyperamazing it might be, on *The Metamorphosis of Iris's Bum into a Star* is no longer sufficient for that; it's necessary to write a history in fifty volumes of the Ducs de Castelnaudry, to have pierced a number of isthmuses, translated Greenlandish novels, to be a bishop, an admiral, or at least a veterinarian.

My ambition is not so high . . . oh, triple idiot that I am! My ambition is a thousand times higher, since it goes so far as begging your generosity, Madame, for the alms of a quarter of an hour of indulgent attention and the signal favor of a quarter of a smile on your lips!

And then, thinking about it, what's the point of all this? What's the point of all these absurd prolegomena, which are doubtless boring you? Will people not say, truly, that my story is quite terrible? As terrible as the things that are, as you know, said between men at the end of dinners?

Not at all. It isn't a matter of such horrors. When this lewd story was told to me, we were not, I swear to you, between men, since it is Chonchinette herself who narrated it. It's true that little Chonchinette is quite a lad, and wear socks—yes, socks, and short hair—like a man, but I swear to you that she doesn't put on trousers. In any case, all that's unimportant, isn't it? One more word, however, a word that will tranquilize you definitively. Let your modesty sleep in peace, Madame. All these oratory precautions are merely futile games to amuse me with your untimely emotion. Let your modesty sleep in peace, for I have bought, a long time ago, in order to draw a veil,

as they say, over the overly cynical verbiage of this accursed tale, several meters of tarlatan, and I swear to you,
I swear to you by all that I hold sacred, on Chonchinette's
snowy tits, that I shall dress the most scandalous item in
this story chastely, in the most prudish of tutus . . .

So here it is.

The scene is happening in New York, at about
two o'clock in the morning, in a private room in a
restaurant.

The debris of victuals are strewn on the table-cloth,
and champagne bottles are lined up, desperately empty.

The apples of his cheeks carmine, he is sitting with his
head tilted back and the nape of his neck on the back of
the armchair, full of a slightly drunken amorous bliss.

Astride his knees, laughing, with her eyes unusually
shiny, She is amusing herself pinching his cheeks, tug-
ging his moustache and blowing in his nostrils. From the
skirts tucked up by the mischievous straddling of the
female—whom, you will have divined, is none other than
Chonchinette herself—emerges the end of a leg, the end
of a leg clad in a sock, a bright blue sock, the end of a
leg that is swinging, back and forth, back and forth . . .
He, stimulated, places an avid caressing hand on the pale
nudity of the calf. The hand climbs . . . The knee . . .

Here, I make it a duty to keep my solemn engagements
by placing a few meters of tarlatan, prudish tarlatan!

The gesture was brief. But, seizing that rascal
Chonchinette in his arms, who struggled—for form's sake,
and not very much—and who laughed, and laughed, the
laugh of a tickled woman, he, quivering with desire, carried her to the divan, the large divan of nacarat velvet.

Then, as he was meticulous, he bounded to the door with the evident intention of shooting the bolt.

But then, O stupor, scarcely has he put his fingers on the handle of the bolt than, moved by an ingenious mechanism—oh, these Americans!—a placard surges forth from the wall, like the prophetic hand at Belshazzar's Feast, a black notice, on which these words are traced in flamboyant golden letters:

Do not employ table linen; there are napkins in the chest of the divan.

For a long time, oh, a very long time, Chonchinette laughs at that!

What? You're not laughing? Madame is indubitably an exquisite lectrice, you're not laughing? You're grimacing, a little moue of disillusion? Oh, I get it! You haven't understood? You don't speak English? No?

Well, neither do I.

THE LOVER

WHEN I returned from the Hindu lands, where I had loved the daughters and wives of rajahs as beautiful as simulacra of new bronze or cornelian in fabulous palaces with golden roofs, walls of jasper, paving stones of ruby, amethyst and chalcedony . . .

When I returned from the mysterious provinces of China, where, for a long time, I had caressed by moonlight, in a fantastic garden full of polycephalous statues, blue eucalypti, painted porcelain turrets and peach-blossom, the little princess with the turned-up eyes, the minuscule feet of a doll, the little princess who was none other than the precious and dear child of the Celestial Emperor . . .

When I had returned from Cytherean azures where, on a bed of pink roses, the divine Aphrodite, more dazzling than the genius of Praxiteles sculpted her, had offered herself to my kisses many times . . .

When I had returned to these sunless climes, obedient to the most bizarre of crazy fantasies, I wanted to choose, among all the women who are for sale, my mistress: very thin, very small, with big blue eyes bitten by the acid of old tears.

I wanted my mistress to have big blue eyes bitten by the acid of old tears, because such eyes are exceedingly diaphanous and I like to contemplate, in the depths of the limpid lake of my beloved's gaze, her soul, her woman's soul, a cloaca of all malevolence and all corruption.

I have chosen my very small mistress in order to give me the childish illusion of a more intimate and more entire possession, in order to be able to enfold her more completely in a single embrace, and to say to myself, infatuated with mad pride: Your arms are vast enough to embrace a universe of felony and egotism.

I have chosen my very thin mistress in order to feel, in the midst of our ardent kisses, the nails of her vertebrae and the trellis of her ribs, and thus to remind myself, in accomplishing the work of life, that the grimacing skeleton of death is lying in wait and watching, eternally hidden beneath our skin.

Thus I wanted to choose my lover, when I returned from the Hindu lands, where I had loved the daughters and wives of rajahs as beautiful as simulacra of new bronze or cornelian in fabulous palaces with golden roofs, walls of jasper, paving stones of ruby, amethyst and chalcedony.